George M. Baker

**The Exhibition Drama**

comprising drama, comedy, and farce, together with dramatic and musical

entertainments, for private theatricals, home representations, holiday and school

exhibitions

George M. Baker

**The Exhibition Drama**
*comprising drama, comedy, and farce, together with dramatic and musical entertainments, for private theatricals, home representations, holiday and school exhibitions*

ISBN/EAN: 9783337288013

Printed in Europe, USA, Canada, Australia, Japan

Cover: Foto ©Andreas Hilbeck / pixelio.de

More available books at **www.hansebooks.com**

# THE EXHIBITION STAGE

BOSTON: LEE AND SHEPARD.

THE AMATEUR DRAMA SERIES.

THE

# EXHIBITION DRAMA:

COMPRISING

DRAMA, COMEDY, AND FARCE,

TOGETHER WITH

DRAMATIC AND MUSICAL ENTERTAINMENTS,

FOR

*PRIVATE THEATRICALS, HOME REPRESENTATIONS, HOLIDAY AND SCHOOL EXHIBITIONS.*

BY

## GEORGE M. BAKER,

Author of "Amateur Dramas," "The Mimic Stage," "The Social Stage,"
"The Drawing-Room Stage," "Temperance Dramas," "A Baker's
Dozen," "Humorous Dialogues," "Running to Waste,"
&c.

Illustrated.

BOSTON:
LEE AND SHEPARD, PUBLISHERS.
NEW YORK:
LEE, SHEPARD, & DILLINGHAM.
1875.

BOSTON:

RAND, AVERY, & CO., STEREOTYPERS AND PRINTERS.

# PREFACE.

———◆———

In the preparation of "The Exhibition Drama," the author has endeavored to present as great a variety as in the previous volumes of this series, and to comply, as far as possible, with the requests of numerous correspondents. Thus "Enlisted for the War" was written in response to a demand for something, based on the late civil war, which should meet the requirements of various Posts of the G. A. R. The musical allegories, "The Visions of Freedom," and "The Tournament of Idylcourt," were prepared for the graduating-class in a Boston grammar-school, and are of the same general character as those previously issued. The Christmas entertainment, and the dramatization of Dickens's "Christmas Carol," have both been successfully performed at sabbath-school entertainments. These, as well as the allegories, are plentifully supplied with tableaux, easily represented, and are adapted to the wants of many occasional exhibitions.

That "Amateur Dramas" are successful, the appearance

of a fifth volume is convincing testimony. In addition to this, the warm commendations of the press, frequent testimonials from public teachers, and last, though not least, a steadily increasing demand for the old as well as the new, convince the author that he is honorably catering to a healthy appetite for innocent and wholesome recreation.

G. M. B.

207 WEST SPRINGFIELD STREET, BOSTON.

# CONTENTS.

———◆———

All the above are published separately, and can be obtained of LEE & SHEP-ARD, Publishers, Boston. Price 15 cts. each.

# ENLISTED FOR THE WAR;

or,

## THE HOME-GUARD.

# ENLISTED FOR THE WAR;

OR,

## THE HOME-GUARD.

---

### A DRAMA IN THREE ACTS.

*Also a complete two-act drama, by omitting the second
act, and two characters.*

---

### CHARACTERS.

ROBERT TRUEWORTH, a Soldier of the Union.
WILDER ROWELL, Guardian of Gaylie Gifford.
HOSEA JENKS, Auctioneer.
HIRAM JENKS, his Son, "a mere boy."
CRIMP, Colored.
GEN. GRANT.
LIEUT.-COL. BOXER.
GAYLIE GIFFORD, an Heiress.
MRS. TRUEWORTH, Robert's Mother.
MATTIE TRUEWORTH, Robert's Sister

---

### COSTUMES.

ROBERT.  Acts 1 and 2, Uniform of a private.  Act 3, Uniform of
a colonel.
ROWELL.  Act 1, Modern dress, change to colonel's uniform.  Act
2, Colonel's undress uniform.  Act 3, Fashionable dress.

HOSEA.   Act. 1, Make up "fat;" blue coat with brass buttons; nankeen pants; striped vest; white necktie; face florid; nose a little pimply; curly gray wig.   Act 3, Something like the same, but figure rather emaciated; cheeks sunken; and a little more bald than in first act.

HIRAM JENKS.   Act 1, Short jacket, through which his arms protrude; light pants, very short; blue stockings; thick shoes; crop wig; general juvenile appearance.   Act 3, Short dress bob-tail coat, &c.; not dandified, but neat; should be an entire change from Act 1.

CRIMP.   Act 1, Black woolly wig; gray pants; white shirt, sleeves rolled up; wide-rimmed straw hat.   Act 2, Disguise of an old darkey; gray wig; gray side-whiskers; blue shirt; white duck pants, with one suspender.   Act 3, Black coat and pants; white vest; white necktie.

GEN. GRANT.   Uniform of major-general, with cloak; military slouch hat, full beard, and make up as usual.

GAYLIE GIFFORD.   Act 1, Neat travelling-suit.   Act 3, Handsome evening-dress.

MRS. TRUEWORTH.   Black dress, white collar and cuffs, and widow's cap, very neat.

MATTIE.   Act 1, Muslin dress and white apron; sleeves rolled up.   Act 3, Evening dress

---

NOTE. — "ENLISTED FOR THE WAR," here presented in its most simple form, can be elaborately produced, if preferred. Where a military display is desirable, the second act will allow of "an awkward-squad drill," "relieving guard," a bayonet-drill, or the introduction of a camp song.   At the end of the third act, the returning company might march across the stage, behind windows and door, illuminated with white and red lights, with the chorus "Marching through Georgia."

ACT I. — SCENE. *Interior of farm-house. Door in flat, R. C. Window in flat, L. C. Outside the window arrange flowers in pots, and shrubbery. Inside, muslin curtain draped up at L. Window open; between it and door, bureau or secretary. Lounge or sofa, L. Rocking-chair, R. C. Small table with a chair beside it, L. C.; writing-materials on table. Chair, L. MRS. TRUEWORTH discovered in rocking-chair, knitting and rocking. MATTIE in chair beside table, her arms folded on table, her face hidden in her arms.*

*Hosea (outside).* It's a downright shame. Look at it ; a fine piece of property like this going, going at such a ruinous sacrifice ; and I'm only offered nine hundred and fifty dollars for it; literally flowing with milk and honey. Shall I have ten, — ten, do you say? Quick, or you lose it : nine hundred and fifty once, nine hundred and fifty twice, nine hundred and fifty, — going, going, and gone to Wilder Rowell, Esq., for nine hundred and fifty dollars. You've got a bargain.

*Mattie (raising her head).* Do you hear, mother? To Wilder Rowell.

*Mrs. T.* It's a shame to let it go for that price, and to a stranger.

*Mattie.* Mr. Rowell is no stranger, mother. It's now five years since he came to Grainlow with Mr. Gifford.

*Mrs. T.* For all that, he's a stranger, — a proud,

haughty man, whom nobody likes, nobody has confidence in.

*Mattie.* Mr. Gifford had confidence enough to give him the guardianship of his daughter when he died two years ago; and Gaylie likes him. As for being proud and haughty, to me he is always pleasant and condescending.

*Mrs. T.* Condescending, indeed! You're just as good as he is. Bless you, child, the Trueworths held their heads as high as the best of folks until our troubles commenced. Your father took to borrowing to experiment with his patent wrinkles, and mortgaged the farm to that mean skinflint, Hosea Jenks. Ah, well! he did it for the best, no doubt. Only six months dead, and now the old farm has gone too.

*Mattie.* Mother 'tis hard, 'tis cruel, to leave you homeless in your old age. Had father been wise —

*Mrs. T.* Hush, child! not a word against him. He was a good, kind father, and a husband to be proud of. In all his troubles he never would touch a cent of the money we had put by to push Rob through college. That was safely locked up; and the lad came through with all the honors.

*Mattie.* What good can his learning do him now?

*Mrs. T.* That remains to be seen. When the call came for men, our boy, bless him! stepped out with the first, and enlisted for the war. Then came the hard blow, hardest of all to bear. My own dear, noble husband breathed out his life in my arms, and joined the true and noble in that better land. Hark! I hear Robert's step. (MATTIE *rises, and goes up* to the window. ROBERT *enters slowly door in flat; comes down, places his hand on the back of his mother's chair.*)

*Rob.* Mother, the farm has gone. We are homeless.

*Mrs. T. (wipes her eyes, and endeavors to suppress emotion).* Yes, Rob, the old home is ours no more. Perhaps it is as well we made a change. Now he who, who (*rises, and stretches out her arms*) — O Rob, Rob! I can't bear it; I can't bear it. (*Sobs, and falls upon his neck.*)

*Rob (embracing her).* O mother! this should not have been. Had I known the worst, I could have prevented it. I have strong arms and a cool head. I could have managed the farm. I thought father was so comfortably settled; and now my enlistment binds me. Oh, I could have done bravely!

*Mrs. T. (recovering).* And you will do bravely now, where every true man should stand in the hour of his country's peril, in the ranks of brave defenders. Fear not for us: there's a power of strength in these old arms yet, and a stout heart to struggle; ay, and a brave one. Am I not the mother of a man who leaves all to serve his country?

*Rob.* Brave mother, you shall have a son to be proud of.

*Mrs. T.* Right, boy. And my prayers and blessing shall cheer you on to victory.

*Rob.* Yet you are homeless, mother. Our regiment is ready for the field: it only awaits the appointment of a colonel. I may be called away at an hour's notice. If I could only have secured the old home for you, I should have been content.

*Mattie.* Rob, why did you not ask the assistance of Gaylie Gifford? She is rich, and I know would have helped us. — her old home too.

*Rob.* Yes, her old home. Dear little girl! how fond we all were of her, and she of us! But she went away to school two years ago. perhaps has forgotten us.

*Mrs. T.* Why, Rob, not a week passes but I have a letter from her; such a good, kind letter too!

*Rob.* Yes, I know; and yet I could not *ask* her assistance.

*Mattie.* Perhaps you are right, Rob; but it does seem hard, after all the care and attention she has received from mother, she could do nothing for us. But they do say money makes inward changes as well as outward. Thank Heaven, we're out of its temptation!

[*Exit* R.

*Rob* (*seating his mother in her chair, and kneeling at her side*). Mother, there's one reason why I could not ask Gaylie for assistance. I should like to tell you, for I would want her to know it should I never return.

*Mrs. T.* Never return! O Rob! do not say that.

*Rob.* That is one of the chances of war, mother. We must think of it. 'Tis the unlucky chance in this game of life, when so much depends on my success. But Gaylie, mother.

*Mrs. T.* Well, Rob, what of Gaylie?

*Rob.* Mother, you will, perhaps, call me mad; but, since Gaylie left us, a wild and strong desire has taken possession of my heart. I could not see her growing up so good and beautiful, without becoming more and more strongly attached to her. At college my dreams were of her; my waking thoughts again and again fashioned her image into dear companionship; and I have at last dared to believe that I might one day woo her, perhaps win her.

*Mrs. T.* Rob, my boy, 'tis a wild dream. She is a rich heiress; in a year will be mistress of that grand estate yonder. (*Enter door in flat* WILDER ROWELL.)

*Rob.* Yes, mother; but I am a soldier of the Union; and, out of that glorious majority who are to battle for its rights, the North will pick its trusty leaders. Why may not I rise? Why may not I win rank and glory? and, when that is gained, why may not I dare to ask the hand of her I love so dearly, Gaylie Gifford?

*Rowell* (*at back*). I beg your pardon if I intrude. (*Rob rises.*) Mr. Jenks asked me to step inside. He will soon join me to complete the sale.

*Mrs. T.* (*rising*). You are in your own house, sir. 'Tis we who intrude.

*Rob.* Mr. Rowell, I shall take immediate steps to find another home for my mother and sister. We will not long trespass.

*Rowell* (*down* L.). Oh, take your own time: perhaps 'twill not be necessary to remove.

*Rob.* How? I do not understand you.

*Rowell.* I will speak with you again: for the present, make yourself perfectly at home in my house.

*Rob* (*aside*). His house. Poor old house! you have fallen among thieves. Come, mother. (*Puts his arm about his mother's waist, and they exeunt* R. Row-

ELL *looks after them, then places his hat on bureau at back, and sits at table.*)

*Rowell.* Well, I certainly have heard something to my advantage. So, my fine soldier-boy, you love my ward, Gaylie Gifford. So do I. There we are perfectly agreed. But, when it comes to possession, I think we shall quarrel. Forewarned, forearmed. I have purchased this farm for the purpose of pleasing my ward; well knowing, that, had she been informed of the sale, she would have requested its purchase, that in gratitude she might have restored it to her old protectress. Her gratitude to me, for my wise forethought, would, no doubt, bring me one step nearer to my ambition. But this soldier loves her; should she be allowed to carry out her wishes, would love her all the more, perhaps arouse an answering affection. No. I'll keep the farm for my own pleasure; perhaps play the *rôle* of benefactor myself. Gaylie's large fortune must be shared with me. I never dreamed of this fellow's ambition. He rise? If fortune only smile upon me, I will guard against that.

*Crimp* (*outside*). I'm obleeged to you. Massa Jinks. I jes w-w-want to know w-w-w-whar you gwine t-t-t-ote dis yere farm?

*Hosea* (*outside*). Oh, bother! do you suppose we're going to dig it up, and cart it off, you stupid? (*Enter door in flat, followed by* CRIMP.)

*Crimp.* S'pose, s'pose; donno nuffin 'bout s'posin, Massa Jinks. You cum down here, Massa Jinks, betwixt eleben and seben, A.M., into de forenoon. You stick up a red frag ober de do', and you gets up onto de barril; and, when you's onto de barril, you gets a crowd round de barril, and deliber a Fourfe-ob-July speech onto de barril, and you jaw away, and ax 'em for dollars, nine hundred dollars, fify dollars, and tell dat ar assemblin' dis yere farm am gwine, gwine, gwine; and all I ax you for to tole me, whar it am gwine for to go. I'm obleeged to you.

*Hosea.* Oh! that's only a figurative expression. I've sold the farm: that's all.

*Crimp.* Figger-who? Sole de farm; who tole you? who ax you?

*Hosea.* My interest.

*Crimp.* In-ter-which? who's he?

*Hosea.* I had a mortgage on the property, fore-closed, and sold out.

*Crimp.* M-m-m-orgages onto de property. No, sar, don't raise 'em; heaps ob cabbages, but no morgages. I'm obleeged to you.

*Hosea.* Well, I've sold the property, — house, land, farming-utensils, and live stock.

*Crimp.* Live stock; horses, cows, by golly, and de hogs (*Hosea nods*), and de chickens and roosters?

*Hosea.* Yes, sold them all.

*Crimp.* By golly, you don't mean it; w-w-w-what we gwine to do for Fanksgibben? And de ole ram Jim, — he gwine too?

*Hosea.* Yes, the old ram Jim.

*Crimp.* Golly, dat so? I'm obleeged to you, Massa Jinks. Dat are ole ram Jim am de mos' dys-peptic biped —

*Hosea.* Quadruped, Crimp. Bipeds walk on two legs: he goes on four.

*Crimp.* Does he, Massa Jinks? You jes' don't know ole Jim: by golly, he's on two legs mos' de time, and gwine for me so (*imitates butting*), see, so. Hope I may die, Massa Jinks, if dat ar ole Jim didn't creep up a-hind me las' night when I was a-leanin' ober de pig-sty, jes' as easy, and lif' me ober dat ar fence into de mud, afore you could ax no questions. Nearly took away my bref. I'm glad he's gwine ; he's too sociable ; he is always teasin' folks to take a horn wid him. always wantin' to help gib you a boost. By golly, I's glad ole Jim gwine.

*Hosea.* Suppose you go and tell him so.

*Crimp.* What, me? Guess not, Massa Jinks. We ain't on speakin' terms ; de conbersation am always interrupted wid so many buts. can't get on at all. But I'll jes' go and gib him a hint, Massa Jinks, — wid a stone. By golly, ole Jim gwine ! Hi ! de jubilum am come. I'm obleeged to you.                [*Exit* F.

*Hosea.* Now, Mr. Rowell, I'm at your service ; sorry to have kept you waiting.

*Rowell.* It's of no consequence, Jenks : by the way, Miss Mattie Trueworth is a very pretty girl.

*Hosea.* Isn't she? If she only went with the farm you'd get the *true worth* of your money. You see : ha, ha, ha ! I'm always doing it : can't help it : will pop out in my office, at my table. even in my dreams. It's a bad habit, — a *punicious* habit, for which I ought to be punished. There it is again ! Ha. ha, ha ! I can't help it. I try, but it's no use ; in my office, at my table —

*Rowell.* I'm to pay you one hundred dollars.

*Hosea.* Exactly, to bind the bargain; balance in ten days.

*Rowell* (*takes out pocket-book*). These Trueworths are evidently in a bad way.

*Hosea.* Very. Farm gone, all gone. Poor folks! my heart bleeds for them.

*Rowell.* Does it, indeed? The farm is sold to pay your claim.

*Hosea.* Yes, and you've got a bargain. It's war-times, and folks ain't a-goin' to put out their money. A year ago, three thousand dollars could not have bought this farm. What's the use of buying land when there's no telling but what the Southern Confederacy will sweep every thing afore the war's over?

*Rowell.* Indeed! then you've not much faith in the success of Northern arms?

*Hosea.* It does look a leetle black for the North.

*Rowell.* If that's your opinion, perhaps I'd better withdraw before the bargain's closed.

*Hosea.* What! back out? Don't you do it! It's always blackest just afore day. The right must conquer: it's a magnificent farm. It's only a question of time: a hundred dollars if you have it ready. The Union must be preserved: best cows in the country. Look at the uprising: a million freemen in arms, — ninety acres of meadow-land. — marching on to victory. And we're so far north, you know, it's a safe investment. I'll write a receipt.

*Rowell* (*throws down money, and rises*). There's your money.

*Hosea.* That's good. (*Snatches the money.*) The

best investment you ever made. (*Sits and writes.*)
There's your receipt. Thank you. (*Rises and shouts.*)
Hi, sonny, take down the flag: bargain's closed.
That's my son out there; a mere boy, but awful smart
if he's kept in his place. Hiram Jenks is his bap-
tismal name. I call him Hi, for short: see the pun?
ha, ha, ha! Hi Jenks, when I'm in a highly humorous vein, — that's another; and when he's in a teas-
ing humor, I call him Hi, son. There's another! Ha,
ha, ha! Can't help it: I'm always doing it. I must
be funny; in my office, at my table —

*Rowell.* You seem to be a very busy man, Mr.
Jenks.

*Hosea.* I am. I'm a auctioneer, funeral under-
taker, coroner, lawyer, expressman, carpenter, shoe-
maker, any thing by which I can gain an honest penny.
There's only one office that seems necessary to my
happiness. I would be a postmaster; and Stamps is
on his last legs. Poor fellow! he's nearly stamped
out of existence. You see: ha, ha, ha! I can't help
it; it will pop out. Perhaps it's better, for humor is
dangerous when it strikes in. See? Ha, ha, ha!

*Rowell.* Your humor is not of the strikin' kind,
Mr. Jenks.

*Hosea.* Ha, ha, ha! very good; it's catching.
Strike in: that's (*looks grave*) rather good.

*Rowell.* There's a son at the head of this Trueworth family, I believe?

*Hosea.* Yes; a splendid fellow, who enlisted a
week before his father died. Poor chap! he's awfully
cut up. Thought the old folks nicely settled, and was

chock full of patriotism. Was disappointed in that, but could not get out of Uncle Sam's clutches. I couldn't afford to lose my money. so foreclosed and sold out. (*Enter door in flat* Hiram Jenks *with a long pole, on which a red auction-flag is rolled, on his shoulder.*)

*Rowell.* 'Twas a hard blow for the family. (Hiram *turns to shut the door: pole swings round, and hits* Hosea *in the head.*)

*Hosea.* Oh, murder! you clumsy chap, you've broke my head.

*Hiram.* 'Twas a hard blow for you, dad, — an auctioneer knocked down under his own flag.

"When pole meets poll, then comes the crack of skull."

*Hosea.* Shut up, sonny! Where's your manners? Hold up your head. (*Hiram obeys the directions as spoken.*) Boys should be seen, not heard. Turn out your toes. That was good, though, "when pole meets poll:" ha, ha, ha! He can't help it: takes it from me. I can't help it; in my office, at the table —

*Rowell.* I'm anxious to settle this business at once, and get possession of the farm. If you will arrange the papers, my check is ready to-day for the whole amount of purchase.

*Hosea.* I like that. My son. hold up your head: here's an example for you: a man who's anxious to pay, — turn out your toes. — who never puts off until tomorrow what can be done to-day. When you grow up, sonny, remember ready is the color of the winning

horse on the racecourse of life, — Ready-cash; by
whom that *dun*-colored nag Promise-to-pay is always
distanced. Ha, ha. ha! There's a pair of 'em. I
can't help it; it will pop out; in my office, at my
table —

*Rowell.* I'm in something of a hurry.

*Hosea.* All right: step over to my office, and we'll
settle up at once. Sonny, straighten up! You are
released from official business, and may go off fishing.
(*Pats him on the head.*) That's good. Ha, ha, ha! I
can't help it; 'twill pop out regardless of time and
place. We wits know no pent-up Utica. You take,
hey, Rowell? Ha, ha, ha! I really can't help it; in
my office, at my table —

*Rowell.* Mr. Jenks, I really must insist —

*Hosea.* You can't stand it. hey? Then we'll move
on. Sonny. stand by the flag. I'm going, going,
gone. Ha, ha, ha! [*Exit, followed by* ROWELL, *door
in flat.*]

*Hiram* (*stands c., and looks after them*). Sonny,
sonny! Well, if the old man keeps on his degenerating pace, he'll be in his second childhood in six
months. Calls me a boy, a mere boy: twenty last
month. Keeps me in a short jacket, and shorter pantaloons. Makes me keep my hair sandpapered like an
urchin of ten. It's about time this thing was stopped.
If my arm creeps through this jacket much farther,
I'm very much afraid it will rise in indignation. and
smite my aged sire. "Honor your parents" is a very
good maxim, but it may be carried a little too far.
I'd go into the army, but he won't let me; swears I

shall stand by the old flag. (*Clasps the auction-flag in his arms.*) No matter: it's only a year, and I am free. Ah! here's Mattie Trueworth, a girl I would lay down my life for, and who laughs at me. Heigho! if I wasn't a boy, I should be very much in love with her. How d'ye do, Mattie? (*Enter* MATTIE R.)

*Mattie.* Oh! it's you, Hiram Jenks.

*Hiram.* Yes, it's me, Mattie; the standard-bearer, (*pompously*) bearing the old flag. that has conquered in so many battles; under whose folds so many household gods have fallen, never to rise again.

*Mattie.* Pshaw! you'd look more manly bearing the flag of your country.

*Hiram.* S'pect I would, Mattie: it's what I'd like. But dad says No.

*Mattie.* Oh, indeed! a dutiful son, truly. The house is sold: why do you wait here?

*Hiram.* To get a word with you, Mattie. I've a great admiration for you. If I dared, I would tell you that I love you. (*Places flag in* R. *corner back.*)

*Mattie.* Don't you dare do any such thing. You must know I detest you, a mere boy; why, you're not yet out of jacket and trousers!

*Hiram* (*stretching up his arms*). You're mistaken, Mattie: I'm a long way out of them.

*Mattie.* Hiram Jenks, you're a fool.

*Hiram.* That's just what dad says, Mattie; but he's awfully mistaken. He's old and queer, so I think it no harm to humor his fancies, though I do get laughed at. He does not know, that, long after he's asleep, the fool is studying by candle-light, way into the night ; that, while he's about his business, the fool's ears are open, and his eyes sharp set, watching the kinks and tricks of trade. Only a year, Mattie, and I shall be free, — free to laugh at him, free to win you.

*Mattie.* Win me! Hiram Jenks, have you lost your senses?

*Hiram.* Sometimes I think I have, Mattie, when I look at you. Don't be hard on me. Think me a boy, if you will : only remember that I love you dearly ; for your sake, would die a thousand deaths.

*Mattie.* What unparalleled devotion ! (*Sits in chair* R., *and turns her back.*)

*Hiram.* Mattie, Rob must soon leave for the battle-field. You will then need a friend. Let me take his place, be a brother to you ; or give me the right to be nearer and dearer. (*Kneels, and takes her hand.*) Speak, Mattie : I love you dearly, truly. (*Enter door in flat* HOSEA, *followed by* ROWELL.)

*Hosea.* Good gracious, boy ! what are you about? You're spoiling your trousers. (HIRAM *jumps up.*) Mattie, don't let that boy pester you with his nonsense. Sonny, go home. (*Aside.*) 'Pon my word, I believe the boy was making love to that girl. I must look after him a little closer. (*Aloud.*) Hiram, hold up your head, turn out your toes, 'bout face, march ! (HIRAM *looks at his father as if he would defy him, then obedi-ently marches off.*) Now, Mr. Rowell, you are in pos-session. There is the deed (*giving paper*), where you may read your title clear. *What's* to prevent? Ha, ha, ha ! there it is again ! I can't help it ; in my office —

[*Exit* D. *in* F.

*Rowell.* Miss Mattie, will you be kind enough to inform your brother that I would speak with him?

*Mattie (rising).* Certainly, sir. He's somewhere about the place: I'll find him. [*Exit* R.

*Rowell.* I will make an attempt to dispose of this farm to advantage. I must be quick: Gaylie is expected home to-day, may return at any moment. If this fellow was only out of the way, 'twould be clear sailing. Yet if I can manage to spike his guns before the prize heaves in sight, the victory is mine. (*Sits at table. Enter* R. ROB.)

*Rob.* You would speak with me, Mr. Rowell?

*Rowell.* Yes: take a chair. (*Rises, and offers chair to* ROB, *then goes* L., *and brings chair to* L. *of table:* both sit.) This farm has passed from the possession of your family into my hands; the purchase-money is all paid; and I now hold by right the title-deed. Here it is. (*Lays it on table.*)

*Rob.* I understand. Your property shall be vacated at once.

*Rowell.* Not so fast, my dear fellow: hear me out. You are a brave man; you have enlisted in your country's cause. You must go to the battle-field, and leave your dear ones to the tender mercies of this little world. I cannot be insensible to such patriotism, and I would befriend you in this emergency.

*Rob.* You befriend me! I have no claim upon you.

*Rowell.* But you have upon my ward. She was reared beneath this roof. Were she here, I think she would uphold me in what I am about to do, — restore to you this farm.

*Rob.* Restore it! I have no right to it. 'Tis yours by lawful purchase.

*Rowell.* You're right; and as an act of justice to one who gives himself to a great cause, that his dear ones shall not be left helpless, I give you back the farm.

*Rob.* You do this, Mr. Rowell: you give me the farm freely, unconditionally?

*Rowell.* Not exactly. There is one condition, and only one. (MATTIE *appears at window outside, with a pair of scissors, and is arranging and clipping her flowers, overhearing the following dialogue.*)

*Rob.* One condition. Mr. Rowell, before you state that condition. let us understand one another. I do not like you. I have felt an instinctive dislike from the time you first entered this town. I have heard hard stories concerning you, — that you have wronged men, ay, and women too. With all that, I have no right to prevent my mother and sister from remaining in their old home. I will not, can I do so honorably. But I will accept no favor from you. Show me any way in which I can redeem this place, the way to win it back by good service that shall repay in full all expenses you have incurred in its purchase, or encumber it with a mortgage and heavy interest; but give me time to redeem. and I will believe you are my friend, will trust you. Come, I have spoken plainly: now let me hear your condition.

*Rowell.* Ha! I like plain speaking. You are an adept at it. You don't like me. Well, then, in place of favor, I will offer a bargain. Here it is: this farm to you and yours forever, for a promise — a pledge — that you never offer your hand to my ward, Gaylie Gifford.

*Rob.* Gaylie Gifford, — my hand! — Mr. Rowell, you are jesting.

*Rowell.* No, I am serious. When I entered this house for the first time to-day, I heard your confession to your mother. I know how grateful Gaylie is for the kind care bestowed upon her here in childhood; and I would not have her kind heart wounded by the belief that one with whom she has been so intimate should presume upon her friendship, to seek to gain her hand, and with it a fortune.

*Rob* (*rising*). Mr. Rowell, you are insulting.

*Rowell.* Come, be reasonable! You can never hope to win her. Give me your promise, and the farm is yours.

*Rob.* No! A thousand times no! You know my secret, but you know not me. I do love Gaylie Gifford, and with a hopeless love. The very fortune you taunt me with seeking is a bar to keep me silent.

*Rowell.* Then take the farm. I will willingly give it up to purchase your silence. She can never be yours: 'twas her father's wish, that, when she became of age, her hand should be given to another.

*Rob.* And that other, yourself. Am I not right, Wilder Rowell?

*Rowell.* 'Twas a pretty shrewd guess.

*Rob.* It is a lie. He had no such wish. My father was with him when he died.

*Rowell* (*rising*). Lie! this to me?

*Rob.* Ay, a lie! You like plain speaking. I know he left her free to choose her own mate, and bade you, as her guardian, to respect her choice.

*Rowell.* I am her choice. Already she trusts me, with a confidence that only love can bring; and I, I love her, dearer than all else in the world.

*Rob.* Except her fortune. You love her, Wilder Rowell, and she is in your power. Poor Gaylie! You shall not win her. She is too good, too pure, to mate with such as you, an adventurer, a fortune-hunter.

*Rowell.* Indeed! Come, we are rivals. I will be magnanimous: you shall have the first chance. Speak, tell her of your love. If she says, Yes, I'm silent.

*Rob.* O villain! you know your power. Speak to her, tell her of my love; I a poor soldier, she a rich heiress! She would think me as mercenary as I know you to be. No, no, I cannot: I love her dearly, truly, but must still love on in secret. (*Falls into chair, and buries his face in his hands on table*).

*Rowell* (*rising. Aside*). Honorable to the last! There's no fear of him. (*Aloud.*) Think well of it, Trueworth. Take the farm, and make your dear ones comfortable. The prize you covet hangs too high. (*Aside.*) Silent! I'll look in on him again (*takes deed*): an hour's reflection may awaken a better spirit.

[*Exit door in flat, passing* MATTIE, *who enters.*

*Mattie* (*going to* ROB). Why, Rob, what's the matter?

*Rob.* Nothing, Mattie: I was only thinking over a plan I have for your future.

*Mattie.* Gaylie's back, Rob: I just saw her carriage drive up to the house.          [*Down* R.

*Rob.* Indeed! Then I shall see her before I go. Where's mother? (*Enter* Mrs. Trueworth, R.)

*Mrs. T.* Here, Rob. What had Mr. Rowell to say to you?

*Rob.* Nothing, mother, to benefit us. I must go out, and look about for a new home. Home! home! that's a hard place to find, when the roof that has so long sheltered us is stripped from our heads.

*Mrs. T.* Home is where the heart is, Rob; and, while the old love binds us together, we can bid defiance to adversity, beneath the humblest roof.

*Rob* (C.). That's right, mother. Keep up a brave heart. We shall weather the storm. (*Aside.*) Oh! who will care for these dear ones when I am gone? (*Crosses to* L.)

*Gaylie* (*outside*). Ha, ha, ha. old Jim! you know me, don't you? keep away! Open, locks, whoever knocks. I'm home, I'm home! (*Runs in door in flat.*) Home, home again! You dear, good Mother Trueworth! (*Runs into* Mrs. Trueworth's *arms*, C.; Mattie R., Rob L.)

*Mrs. T.* Dear child, welcome, a thousand times welcome!

*Gaylie.* I knew you'd be glad to see me; and Mattie (*runs to her* R., *and embraces her*), you dear darling. how rosy you look!

*Mattie.* Gaylie, this is a surprise. I'm real glad to see you.

*Gaylie.* Of course you are; isn't it jolly? But where's Rob?

*Rob* (*advancing*). Here he is; patiently waiting to be recognized.

*Gaylie* (*runs to him, and catches his hands, shaking them heartily*). Oh, you dear old fellow! How glad I am to see you! Why don't you kiss me?

*Rob* (*kissing her*). That was certainly an oversight. So you are back again, the same dear, good Gaylie. Two years' schooling has made little alteration in you.

*Gaylie* (c. *with* ROB; MRS. TRUEWORTH *sits in rocking-chair;* MATTIE *stands* L., *with arms akimbo*). Yes, it has. I'm spoiled, completely spoiled. Got a beau yet, Mattie?

*Mattie.* No, indeed! I hope not.

*Gaylie.* Ha, ha, ha! what a girl! sneers at her destiny. She'll get over it. Yes, I'm completely spoiled. Went away a *cheild* of nature, fresh, buoyant, and all that sort of thing: I've come back a cultivated woman. Ahem! (*Struts across stage: comes back.*) Oh, my poor little head! it's had Latin squeezed into it, Greek pounded into it, and French, German, Spanish, and Italian filtered through it. Oh, it's a learned head! Then my fingers have been calloused into familiarity with all the ugly notes in the musical scale; my feet twisted and turned about all the figures a French dancing-master could invent; and my poor little figure tortured with elegant movements and graceful poses. Oh, bless you! I'm not myself at all. (*Goes back to Rob.*)

*Rob.* You are our own Gaylie still. I know it; I can feel it in the warm clasp of your hand, in the clear light of your eyes.

*Gaylie.* Right, Rob: you're always right. For this dear old home, you, my earliest, best friends, are a part of this my heart; and that not all the teaching in the world could change. (*Goes to* Mrs. Trueworth, *and kneels at her side.* Rob *goes up stage, and watches her.*) So here I am again, mother, at your feet. When my father went to that far-off land, years ago, in search of wealth, he left me here, and asked you to be a mother to his child. How well you took the place of her who died when I was so little, let this testify. I am now the heiress to his wealth; I have a home rich and attractive, servants at my call, much that can make life bright and beautiful: but I could part with all, sooner than lose the right to call this home, and you mother.

*Mrs. T.* (*putting her arms about her*). Dear, dear child! You are my own; still the same fresh, warm heart.

*Rob* (*aside*). She's an angel. Had I but the power to call her mine!

*Crimp* (*outside*). Go 'way dar, you Jim! don't yer shake yer head at me. Go' way dar! help! murder! help! (*Tumbles in at door, as if "butted;" jumps up, runs, and shuts door, placing his back against it.*) Go 'way, yer fool! Nobody to hum.

*Rob.* What's the matter, Crimp?

*Crimp.* Dat ole fo-fo, Jim, he will insist on squartin' me to de door, an' I don't want none of his attention. Go 'way, out dar: stop dat knockin' at do'!

*Gaylie.* Oh, here's our black Cupid! Why, Crimp, old friend, aren't you going to speak to me?

*Crimp* (*comes down*). Why, bress my soul! No,

'tain't. Yes, it am : it's Miss Gaylie hersel'. You dear
little honey ! bress us an' save us, am dat yerself?

*Gaylie (taking his hand)*. Yes, it's your old tor-
ment ; home again, and ready for a frolic.

*Crimp*. Wh-wh-at ! bress yer purty face ; yer ain't
grown a mite ; gwine fur a frolic ; climb de yapple-
trees, ride onto de darky's back. Oh, golly ! what
times we did hab, to be sho' !

*Gaylie*. Only give me a chance, Crimp. I'm as
spry as ever.

*Crimp*. What ! would you, dough, ride onto dis year
darky's back? By golly ! I'm obleeged to you. I's
powerful glad to see ye back, honey. Comfort de ole
lady, now Massa Rob gwine fur a sojer.

*Gaylie*. What ! our Rob a soldier?

*Crimp*. Yaas, indeed ! Don't you see de uniform?
gwine along de tramp, tramp, tramp fellars, he am.

*Rob*. Yes, Gaylie, enlisted for the war.

*Gaylie*. But where are your shoulder-straps, your
sword?

*Rob*. I am but a private, Gaylie. The emblems
of command are yet to be won : they'll come in time, I
hope.

*Gaylie*. I know they will. O Rob ! I'm proud of
you.

*Crimp*. Same here, Massa Rob. I'm obleeged to
you. Golly ! if I was only a white man, I'd jist go
down dar, I would. Hi ! I'd lay 'em out. I'd go for
dem are fellars, like ole Jim, so (*butting*). But dey
don't want no brack guards ; oh, no ! S'pect dey will,
dough, glad to git 'em afore de war am ober ; and, when
de do, hi ! Tumms Jeff'sum Crimp am dare, he am.

*Rob.* It strikes me, Crimp, you are rather monopolizing the conversation. Fall back, sir.

*Crimp.* I'm obleeged to you, Massa Rob. I's dumb. (*Goes to window, and in dumb show pesters the imaginary* JIM *by shaking his fist, throwing things out of the window, &c.*)

*Rob* (L. C.). Yes, Gaylie, I am expecting daily orders to march. I only hope I shall have time to completely settle mother and Mattie in their new home.

*Gaylie* (R. C.). Their new home! what do you mean?

*Rob.* The farm has been sold, Gaylie, — sold to-day, to satisfy the claim of Hosea Jenks.

*Gaylie.* Sold! Why have I heard nothing of this?

*Rob.* You must have known it. Pardon me: I see I have been mistaken. Your guardian —

*Gaylie.* Has not written me a word concerning you; not a word have I heard of this. But 'tis not too late: the farm can and must be redeemed. Who is the purchaser?

*Rob.* Your guardian, Wilder Rowell.

*Gaylie.* He bought it? then it's all right. Dear, good fellow! he knew I could not desert you. That's just splendid! (*Enter hurriedly*, ROWELL, *door in* F.)

*Rowell.* Miss Gaylie, I have this moment heard of your arrival. Welcome home! (*Gives his hand.*)

*Gaylie* (*eagerly shaking it*). A thousand, thousand thanks, Guardy: you have indeed made me welcome. So, sir, you have a surprise in store for me. Come, disclose it: I am all impatience. It's so splendid to be surprised, when you are all prepared for it!

*Rowell.* A surprise? I do not understand.

*Gaylie.* O Innocence! thy name is Wilder Rowell. But I know your secret. You have bought this farm.

*Rowell.* Yes: a good piece of property, they say.

*Gaylie.* Indeed it is! the very investment I should have proposed. Thank you for your thoughtful consideration. So it's my property?

*Rowell.* No, it's my property. Not as your agent, but for myself, I bought this farm. I mean to settle down, and become a sober, plodding farmer, and, in time, take to myself a wife. (*Looks at* ROB, *who is in* L. *corner.*)

*Gaylie.* Guardy, I *have* been mistaken. But you will sell *me* the farm. Come, you never yet refused me a request : and it is one of the dearest wishes I have, to possess this farm.

*Rowell.* Sorry I cannot oblige you. But, for particular reasons, I would not sell this farm for ten times the money I gave for it.

*Gaylie.* But you are turning from their dear home the best friends I have in the world.

*Rowell.* They are not very much attached to it, Gaylie : for, not an hour ago, 'twas offered them on easy terms.

*Gaylie.* Offered them, by you?

*Rob.* Yes, Gaylie : on terms no honest man could for a moment consider.

*Rowell.* I offer it again. Consider, Robert Trueworth, 'tis you who are driving your family from home.

*Rob.* You have had your answer. Scoundrel!

*Rowell.* That name again!

*Rob.* Ay, again and again! Plead no more, Gaylie. Ask no favors for me or mine, of that man: even from your dear hands, I could never take the fair farm which he has polluted by ownership.

*Rowell.* Robert Trueworth, you shall repent this. (*Comes close to him.*) You are making me your enemy.

*Rob.* I am satisfied. Better open war than false friendship with a heartless foe.

*Gaylie.* No more of this, I beg. You have quarrelled. For my sake, be friends.

*Mattie* (R.). Silence, Gaylie! you know not what you ask.

*Gaylie.* You too, Mattie? What means this mystery? (*They pass to* R., *and converse in dumb show. ROB goes up stage, and passes round to back of his mother's chair, on which he leans, conversing with her, as* HOSEA JENKS *enters, followed by* HIRAM. CRIMP *runs to* HIRAM, *and keeps him back, conversing in dumb show about "JIM;"* CRIMP *going through pantomime, to convey an idea of an attack.* HOSEA *comes down,* C.)

*Hosea* (*speaks as he enters*). Oh, here you are, Rowell! I thought I should find you. I've just been down to the post-office. Poor Stamps has gone. He has distributed his last batch, and been transferred to the dead-letter office. Ha, ha, ha! that's a grave pun; but I can't help it; you know my weakness.

*Crimp.* Weakness? am you got de lumbago, Massa Jinks? Golly! I had de rheumatiz awful, las' winter. Tell you what you do, Massa Jinks: you jis get a poorhouse plaster; only draw a quarter out ob yer pocket, and all de anguish out ob yer back.

*Hosea.* Ha, ha, ha! he little understands my facetious humor.

*Crimp.* Oh, humor! face itches; den clap it onto yer face. Draw out all de pain, and some ob yer cheek too.

*Rob.* Crimp, be silent!

*Crimp.* Ob course, ob course! I'm obleeged to you.

*Rowell.* So Stamps is dead?

*Hosea.* Yes: poor fellow, I grieve for him. Who can take his place? — I should say, his post. Post-master, see? ha, ha, ha! There it is again! I can't help it.

*Rowell.* Mr. Jenks, if you could contrive to drop this jesting humor —

*Hosea.* But I can't. I try, but I can't drop it: it's a drop too much. Ha, ha, ha!

*Crimp.* Ya, ya, ya! dat's good: de ole man's been drinking jes' a drop too much.

*Rowell.* If I understand you, Mr. Jenks, you would be his successor.

*Jenks.* That's just it. I know you have influence. See, here's an official envelope addressed to you, and from the war-office too.

*Rowell* (*snatches and opens it*). For me? Ah, good, good! Jenks, I shall remember you. Now comes my turn. Gaylie, I must home at once: will you go with me?

*Gaylie.* I prefer remaining here.

*Rowell.* As you please. Mr. Trueworth, a word with you. (Rob *advances.*) I give you one more opportunity to embrace my offer. 'Tis the last chance. This fine property for your silence.

*Rob.* I will make no terms with you. When I have won the right, I will speak. (*Turns up stage.*)

*Rowell* (*walking up slowly to door*). When you have won the right: that time will never come. Fool! you have made an enemy of one who can strike deep and well. [*Exit door in* F.

*Hosea.* Rowell, Rowell! don't forget me. I must run after him: there's no time to be lost. Come, Hiram! fall in, or we shall fall out. Ha, ha, ha! [*Exit door in* F.

*Crimp.* Take care, Massa Jinks, you don't fall onto ole Jim's horns! (*Looks out at door.*) By golly, he's a-laying fur him. Dere de go! Go in, ole man; he's a arter ye! By golly, see 'em run: see 'em run! (*Exit.* HIRAM *starts for door, stops irresolutely, and then comes, and stretches himself upon lounge.*)

*Hiram.* It's right comfortable here: I think I'll stop.

*Gaylie* (*aside*). He denies my request. What motive can he have in thus appropriating the property of my friends? I must know more of this. (*Aloud.*) Come, mother, show me to my old room. I want to talk to you: I've so much to say! I shall not tell you what I have bought for you. Such a cap, a perfect beauty! and such a shawl! You'll be the envy of the town.

*Mrs. T.* (*rising*). Dear, dear child! ever thoughtful of my comfort.

*Gaylie.* If I were not. I should not deserve so good a mother. Good-by, Mattie: good-by, Rob! [*Exit with arm about* MRS. TRUEWORTH.]

*Rob.* Good-by, Gaylie. Bless her dear heart! mother will have one friend when I am gone. Now, Mattie, I'll take a look about, and see if there's a poor but neat tenement to be had: I won't be gone long.

*Mattie.* O Rob! where can we go?

*Rob.* Trust all to me, Mattie: I will not leave you homeless. (*Going.*)

*Hiram* (*on sofa*). Sh — sh — sh!

*Rob* (*returning*). Why, Hiram, what's the matter? (HIRAM *rises, walks on tiptoe to the window, looks out, turns, "Sh!" then walks to the door, and performs the same manœuvre; then comes down* C. *on tiptoe, beckoning* ROB *down.*)

*Mattie.* What ails the boy? is he crazy?

*Hiram.* Don't mind me. If the old man should happen about, I'm ruined. But, sh — you want a friend.

*Rob.* Well, Hiram, I am not quite destitute.

*Hiram.* Sh — if I only dared, I could find a friend for you. If I only dared; but I'm such a coward. No matter, I'll take the risk. You know the Widow Smith place?

*Rob.* Yes: 'twas sold at auction six months ago.

*Hiram.* Exactly. Sh — it's mine: I bought it.

*Rob.* You? why, 'twas knocked down to Crane!

*Hiram.* Yes: and Crane crooked his long neck round, and took his cue from me. I bought it: my money paid for it. Never you mind where the money came from; it was an honest purchase. Now you're in trouble: you want a home. Take mine, and welcome; only don't let the old man dream I'm its owner. Crane holds it now; but, when I am free, 'twill be known as my property. Will you have it? Not a cent will I take

for it until the war is over. It's a pretty place: not
much land; but flowers, good gracious! and wood-
bine, why, the front is completely covered. Will you
take it? Quick! the old man will return, and then I
am a boy again.

*Rob* (*takes his hand*). Hiram, you're a man: you
are a true friend. Thank you: I will accept your offer.

*Mattie.* O Hiram! I've treated you shamefully.
Forgive me: I never dreamed you had such a noble
heart.

*Hiram.* I haven't any heart, Mattie: you had it
all long ago. So you'll take the place (*enter Gaylie*
R.), and be my tenant until the war is over. Sh — sh!
not a word!

*Gaylie.* You're too late, conspirators: I have heard
all. Rob, you have found a home?

*Rob.* Yes, Gaylie, thanks to a true friend.

*Hiram.* Sh — not so loud; the old man drops
round mighty sudden.

*Gaylie.* Rob, you have done this without consult-
ing me. Why am I shut out from your counsel?

*Rob.* Ah, Gaylie! you cannot befriend me. You
are not of age, and I will not be indebted to your
guardian.

*Gaylie.* Tell me, why have you quarrelled with my
guardian? What means this enmity between you and
him?

*Rob.* Gaylie, you must not ask me.

*Gaylie.* But I must know: you have no right to
keep it from me.

*Rob.* I cannot tell you, Gaylie. Let it suffice, we

are enemies ; that he would do much to crush me and mine.

*Gaylie.* Let him dare ! I stand between you and him. You go to battle in a noble cause : fear not ; if he has the will to wrong the dear ones you leave behind, I have the power to crush him, and I will. Face the enemy in the South with a brave heart, Rob. Against the enemy here, I will be the Home-Guard.

*Rob.* You, Gaylie? what can you do, little woman ?

*Gaylie.* Woman's work. Think you we will sit idle at home, while husbands, fathers, brothers, are in the field? No! there is work for tender hands and willing hearts. To care for the needy, to protect the helpless, at home ; to heal the wounds, and charm away the pain, in the hospitals, — this is our work : to it I give my whole heart ; my whole fortune, if need be. Henceforth I am the guardian of your mother and your sister. (*Enter* CRIMP *door in flat*). Alone, if need be, I will stand the Home-Guard, a bulwark against adversity.

*Hiram.* You shall not stand alone, Miss Gaylie. They say I'm but a mere boy, but I'm heart and hand with you in this cause.

*Crimp.* Same here. I'm obleeged to you ; I'll be de drum-major in dat ar corpse.

*Gaylie.* See, Rob ; they muster at my call. Home-Guard. attention ! fall in ! (*Stands* L. C. HIRAM *steps up beside her;* CRIMP *up stage next him; form in line up and down stage.* MATTIE *sits in rocking-chair,* R. ; ROB *leans upon the back of her chair.*)

*Rob.* Raw recruits, Gaylie !

*Gaylie.* Yes, almost as raw as those who take the field, Rob. Company, attention!

*Crimp.* Hole on, Miss Cap'n. Whar's de colors? mus' have a frag. Golly, dis year's de ticket. (*Takes auction-flag from corner, and unrolls it*). Dar! look at dat; and, as I's de only pusson ob color in dis yer corpse, I'll be de color-bearer.

*Gaylie.* Attention, company!

*Crimp.* Yes, Missy Cap'n; I's all attention.

*Gaylie.* Eyes right: eyes left: salute! (*They bring their hands to a salute. Enter door in* F. *Row-* ELL, *in full uniform of a colonel.*)

*Rowell.* Ah! what new recruits have we here?

*Gaylie.* Mr. Rowell, what does this mean?

*Rowell.* That an honor for which I have exerted much influence has, at the last moment, been conferred upon me. I am appointed colonel of the 10th. (*Bows, and comes to* L. *corner.*)

*Gaylie* (c.) Rob's regiment, and his enemy at its head! Oh, this is cruel!

*Rob.* He in command! He our colonel! Another blow: fate can do no more. (*Goes up* c.)

*Rowell.* Robert Trueworth, you will join your regiment at once. All furloughs are countermanded. We march at sunrise to-morrow.

*Gaylie* (*aside*). Oh, this is terrible! Rob's bitter foe in command: oh, why have they quarrelled? (*Goes to rocking-chair, and leans upon it.*)

*Rob* (*aside*). To serve under that man, whom I detest! There is no escape. I must submit. There's one comfort: his position takes him away from Gaylie.

(*Enter* Mrs. Trueworth r.*) The time has come, mother. I have orders to join my regiment at once: we march at sunrise. Keep a stout heart, mother. I leave kind friends behind, who will see to it you do not suffer.

*Mrs. Trueworth* (*her arms about his neck*). My brave boy, serve well your country, and do not forget your mother. She gives you up freely, with a prayer that you may be found true to your duty. Heaven bless and keep you, Rob! (*They stand together conversing.*)

*Gaylie.* Mattie, before Rob goes, I must know the meaning of this quarrel between him and my guardian. Why is it kept from me? You must know: I conjure you, as you value my friendship, as you love your brother, speak before 'tis too late.

*Mattie.* O Gaylie! I do know ; for his sake I will speak. You are the cause of this quarrel. Both these men love you.

*Gaylie.* Indeed! Oh, I'm so glad!

*Mattie.* Glad! You should be ashamed of yourself. You can't marry them both.

*Gaylie.* Oh! you don't know what I can, what I will do.

*Rob* (*approaching*). Mattie, sister, good-by.

*Mattie* (*rising, and running into his arms.* Gaylie *slips into her seat, and covers her face*). O brother! so soon? what shall we do without you?

*Rob.* Keep a good heart, sister. You will do bravely. (*Kisses her.* Mattie *goes to her mother,* c. Rob *comes down, looks at* Gaylie, *sighs, and turns up stage.*) Good-by, Crimp. (*Shakes hands.*)

*Crimp.* Good-by, Massa Rob. I'm obleeged to you. You'll come home a drum-major, sartin sure.

*Rob.* Thank you, Crimp. Good-by, Hiram, and thank you for your friendly aid.

*Hiram.* Good-by, Rob. I'll look out for the women-folks, sharp too. (*Rob goes to door.*)

*Gaylie* (*running up stage*). Rob, Rob! you've forgotten me!

*Rob.* True, Gaylie. I had not the heart to say farewell to you. You are so dear —

*Rowell.* This is but tardy obedience.

*Rob.* Ah! you fear me, Col. Rowell, no more than I fear myself. But am I not bound in honor to be silent? Gaylie, farewell: you have been a kind friend to us, will still be to my dear ones when I am gone. Good-by.

*Gaylie.* Rob, is there nothing more you would say to me? (*Looks at him tenderly.*)

*Rob.* Nothing, Gaylie: were you but the poor girl I once thought you; but no, no —

*Gaylie.* Rob, whatever you would have said to the poor girl, say to the rich heiress: there's the same heart here.

*Rowell.* Confusion! is she leading him on to confession?

*Rob.* O Gaylie! am I awake? You give me life; you give me hope: you make me bold to speak. Gaylie, I love you, dearly, truly.

*Gaylie* (*placing her hands on his shoulders*). As dearly and truly as I love you? O Rob! it must be deep and strong.

*Rob* (*clasping her in his arms*). Mine, Gaylie, mine! oh, this is happiness indeed!

*Crimp.* Hi, das a fac. De Union forebcr!

*Rowell.* Girl, are you losing your senses? I forbid this folly.

*Gaylie.* And who are you?

*Rowell.* Your guardian. You shall not throw yourself away upon a common soldier.

*Rob* (*comes down*). A common soldier! True. I glory in my rank. You leap to a command by power and influence. My spurs must yet be won. I am content. Should I rise by merit, no emblems of rank could shed a brighter glow than gleams from the trusty bayonets of Liberty's common soldiers.

*Rowell.* Enough! To your regiment. You forget I am your superior.

*Rob.* No, I do not forget it; and I know what to expect, — hard service, and an enemy in command. I am satisfied, for I have won the victory here. (*Takes Gaylie's hand.*)

*Rowell.* Be not so sure of that. You forget the enemy has a long arm, and it may reach even here.

*Gaylie.* And, if it does, I fear it not.

*Rowell.* Indeed!

*Gaylie.* Ay, indeed, Col. Rowell. You are my guardian, true; but you forget my father's will. In one year I am free: even now I have the power of appeal to two noble men, should you distort your power. I will be mistress of my fortune. I will be free to bestow my hand. With the one, I will protect the homeless; with the other, cheer him at whom you sneer, a common soldier. Deny my right at your peril.

*Rowell.* No more of this. Quit that man's side. I command you, obey me!

*Gaylie.* You command? You forget I am a leader here. I entreat you, in the name of justice, to deal fairly and honorably by this true hero, who leaves all to serve his country, to recognize his right to the hand which I freely give. Come, sir, do we part friends?

*Rowell.* Not on such terms as you offer. (*Crosses to* R.)

*Gaylie.* Then beware! you make yourself my enemy. Already you disgrace the rank you've bought, not won. You have command, and my hero in your power. I have love, wealth, and a loyal heart, that abhors injustice. Against all treachery and deceit, against the wily arts you may contrive to shame my hero, I am the Home-Guard, the firm friend, enlisted for the war.

*Tableau:* ROB *and* GAYLIE, C. ROB *has his right arm about her waist, her left hand in his left; she bends forward, with her right hand outstretched to* ROWELL, R., *defying him.* MRS. TRUEWORTH *sits on sofa,* L., *with her handkerchief to her eyes.* MATTIE *with her hand on her mother's shoulder.* CRIMP, *back* R., *has the flag rolled up, and is menacing* ROWELL *with it.* HIRAM *catches it in his hand as it descends, and holds him back. Slow curtain.*

ACT II. — (*After two years.*) *Headquarters of* COL.
ROWELL *in Virginia. Room in a farm-house.
Door in flat* L., *open; window in flat* R., *open.
Landscape behind, moonlight if possible. Set the
" moon"* L., *so the light will fall through the door
and window. Writing-desk or table, against* R.
*side; writing-materials, a candle to light, a pile of
letters and papers, upon it. Chair in front of this.
Give the scene a military character by placing a stack
of arms in* L. *corner back, a pile of knapsacks in* R.
*corner with an American flag thrown over it; hang
up a drum between the door and window.* ROBERT
*discovered, with musket, on guard outside the door;
passes door and window twice. A " distant" fife
plays, " The Girl I left behind me," through: as it
ceases,* RON *should be at door; he leans against the
doorway* L.

*Rob.* The boys are making merry to-night around
the camp-fire; but that lively air brings only sadness
to me. "The girl I left behind me," two years ago, in
Grainlow, Gaylie Gifford, is still silent. Not a line in
reply to my frequent letters. Has she repented of her
choice? No, I cannot believe that; for my sister
writes me she often speaks of me, longs for my return.
But yet she never writes. Perhaps she has never received mine; 'tis hardly possible, and yet her silence —
Can my enemy, the colonel, be conspiring to keep us
apart? He is base enough to use any means to serve

his purpose. By his orders, the mail is brought here, and inspected by him, before delivery; perhaps, that he may intercept any letters for me. If I could only get a single line from her, I would be content. Oh! I am ground down worse than any slave that tills the earth beneath the overseer's lash. Two years of service, and still a private! I know I have been honorably mentioned many times by my captain; and yet poorer men step above me: and I toil on, fight on, with no hope of promotion. Well, they shall not say I have not done my duty. Will the end never come, and free me from this bondage, give me liberty to turn my steps northward, to seek the star of promise that gleams in Gaylie's eyes? Halt! Who goes there?

*Crimp (comes from* L.*, passes the window, and appears at door speaking).* D-d-d-on't shoot! d-d-d-on't shoot! I's only a poor old darky, Massa Sentenull.

*Rob.* Your business here?

*Crimp.* Pressing b-b-business; d-d-d-on't shoot! Want to see de colonel.

*Rob.* The colonel is absent.

*Crimp.* Den I'll walk into de parlor, take a cheer, and wait for um. D-d-d-on't shoot!

*Rob.* Business. Your pass, uncle.

*Crimp.* Pass: yes, massa, got a pass. Here she am! (*Searches pocket.*) Golly! it am gone. No, here she am! (*Searches bosom.*) Not a pass; had um, sure; hope I may die —

*Rob.* What's that sticking out of your hat?

*Crimp.* Golly, dat's so! (*Takes off hat, paper sticking out of crown*). Put um up dar to keep um safe. (*Hands pass.*)

*Rob* (*examines paper*). The pass is right: pass in. (*Resumes march.*)

*Crimp.* Tole you so. Dar aint no inception about dis chile: he's de sole ob honor. (*Comes down.*) Now, w-w-what's a-gon to be did? Missy Cap'n sends me away down here, in dis yer benighted regium, to bring a letter to Massa Rob. Tote about forty mile afore I find him, and den he's on guard. 'Twon't do to gib him de letter now: these sojer fellars so stiff onto de tictacs, dat if I was to gib him de letter, jes as likely to put de bagonet into me, or blow my head off, as not. No, sar: Crimp don't take no risks in dis yer camplain; no, sar, I'm obleeged to you. I'll wait till he's reliebed. Missy Cap'n say. gib 'im de letter, and den lay round, and see what de colonel was about. I'll hab a smoke (*takes out pipe, lights it*), an' I'll lay round. (*Takes the American flag, and wraps it round him.*) Glory, hallelujah! dat's de warmest cobering dat eber a darkey got into. Yaas indeed. It am de protector ob virtue. Dat's me. (*Takes a knapsack for a pillow.*) I'l jles hab a snooze into de corner, till Massa Rob is reliebed. (*Lies down.*) Hi! das a heap ob comfort in de arms ob Morphine. (*Smokes.*) 'Spect Missy Gaylie tink a heap ob dat ar Massa Rob. Oh, lub, lub! when you got into dat Miss Gaylie's heart, you jist found de warmest place in de whole world. Yaas, indeed! (*Drops pipe.*) Dar going to be some fun, down dar in Grainlow. By golly! de Home Guard am gwine to commence operations. Now, Massa Colonel, mind your eye; for de Home Guard am onto de war-path.

*Rob.* Halt! Who goes there? (LIEUT.-COL. BOXER *enters* L., *passes the window to door.* ROB *salutes.* BOXER *enters.*)

*Boxer.* The colonel away still? Hallo! (*Snuffs the air.*) Tobacco, and pipe-tobacco too! Smoking in my quarters! Bah! who is it? I won't have it. If there's any thing I detest, it's smoking; under my very nose too. Here, sentinel! (ROB *steps inside door.*) Have you been smoking?

*Rob.* I never smoke, sir.

*Boxer.* Right: it's a filthy habit. But somebody's been here with a pipe. Now, mind, no more of it. Let no smokers pass that door. 'Tis a strict order which must be obeyed. That's all. (ROB *salutes, and retires.*) Plague take the fellow, whoever he is! The smoke of battle is inspiring; gunpowder is soothing to the nerves; but tobacco-smoke, bah! it makes me sick. [*Exit* L.

*Crimp* (*raising his head*). By golly! dat ar hossifer am riled. Don't like smoke. He's proficient in a liberal heducation, he am. (*Drops head.* GEN. GRANT *appears* L., *slowly passes window, and crosses to door, is stopped by* ROB.)

*Rob.* Halt!

*Grant.* I have business with the colonel.

*Rob.* The colonel is absent.

*Grant.* Then I will await his return.

*Rob.* Halt! I have my orders. No smokers can enter here. If you would pass, put out that cigar.

*Grant.* Indeed! Your orders are strict. (*Looks at* ROB *keenly, then throws away cigar, and enters.*)

5

BOXER *enters* L., *meeting him*.) Good-evening, colonel.

*Boxer* (*saluting*). Good-evening, general. You have surprised our post. The colonel is absent. Can I be of service?

*Grant* (*sitting in chair, and tilting back against table*). Your sentinel ordered me to throw away my cigar.

*Boxer.* He did? confound him! Here, sentinel! (Rob *steps inside door.*) Do you know what you have done?

*Rob.* Obeyed orders, colonel.

*Grant.* Do you know me, sentinel?

*Rob* (*saluting*). I do, general.

*Boxer.* And didn't you know better—

*Grant.* One moment, colonel. Sentinel, you are the first man that ever dared put out my cigar. You did perfectly right: orders must be obeyed. Your name.

*Rob.* Robert Trueworth.

*Grant.* How long have you been in service?

*Rob.* Two years.

*Grant.* That's all. (*Waves his hand.* Rob *salutes and retires.*) Colonel, your orders are too strict. I cannot talk without a cigar.

*Boxer.* Sorry I have not one to offer you, for I do like to see a man enjoy himself. My orders could not apply to you, general.

*Grant.* Thank you; having permission, I can find the cigar. (*Takes out cigar, and lights it.*) I always go armed. That man at the door,—what is his record?

*Boxer.* Excellent: every inch a soldier; the bravest of the brave.

*Grant.* Two years of service, and still a private?

*Boxer.* Yes, general; although he has been honorably mentioned. (*Coughs.*) (*Aside.*) Confound his nasty cigar! (*Aloud.*) There's not the best of feeling towards him on the part of our colonel. A brave soldier, general, but queer. It seems they quarrelled before entering service. (*Coughs.*) (*Aside.*) Oh, I shall choke! (*Aloud.*) A love-affair, I believe. The private won the girl, and so he's not pushed.

*Grant.* Indeed! the colonel brings his private piques into the battle-field. I rather like this boy. (*Looks round.*) Can't we get out of earshot?

*Boxer.* Certainly; in my room. (*Crosses stage, and then opens door* L.) Walk in, general. (GRANT *rises, and crosses stage.*) We shall be secure from interruption here.

*Grant.* No: it's pleasant outside; let's walk awhile. (*Passes out door off* L., *smoking.*)

*Boxer.* Bah! I foresee a smoky campaign here. (*Following him.*)

*Crimp* (*raising his head*). By golly! dat ar fellar's a high buck. Ain't dey nebber gwine to reliebe dat guard? (COL. ROWELL *appears* R., *passes window to door.* ROB *salutes, he enters.* CRIMP *drops his head.*)

*Rowell.* That fellow's on guard to-night. How I hate him! Rebel bullets come fast and thick, but they never reach him. Pity! I should lose a good soldier, no doubt; but I could spare him. (*Goes to table, and lights candle.*) Here's the mail for my inspection; let me see if there's any thing contraband. (*Examines letters.*) "Robert Trueworth." His sister's handwriting; that shall go through. "Robert Trueworth." Gaylie's hand; detained for the present. (*Places it in his bosom.* ROBERT *is at the window outside, watching him.*) I have managed to keep many sweet morsels from his parched lips. Not a letter of hers shall ever reach him while I have the power to prevent. My guardianship has expired: she has come to her fortune, and yet she loves this man. Not a thought of me; and I love her madly. Ah! what's this? (*Takes letter.*) For me, and — Gaylie's hand! (*Tears it open.*) So, so; at last she thinks of me. (*Reads.*) "Dear Colonel: Pardon my long silence. I have not forgotten you. A business matter which I feel it impossible to adjust makes me bold to ask your assistance. Come to Grainlow at once. I have repented of my rudeness to you, long to see you. If you can obtain a furlough, come; if you cannot, I think I could repay you for the loss of your commission should you feel inclined to resign. Believe me, I am not ungrateful for your former kindness, and earnestly entreat you to return. You shall be made happy here if 'tis in my power. Gaylie." So, so; the wind has changed. There is only one construction to be placed upon that letter. She has repented of her folly, and I can win her. (*Soldier enters* R., *and relieves guard.*) What's that? Ah! relieving guard; I'm glad of that: I cannot bear to have that fellow near me. (ROB *is about to pass off; stands irresolute a moment, then steps inside door. The colonel is again busy with his letters.*)

*Crimp* (*aside*).   Golly! de guard am reliebed.

*Rob* (*removes hat*).   Your pardon, colonel.   Can I speak with you?   *Comes down* L.)

*Rowell* (*turns round*).   Eh? oh, Private Trueworth! Certainly, if it is important.

*Rob.*   You have the mail.   Are there letters there for me?

*Rowell.*   If there are any, they will be forwarded to your company quarters.   (Rob *is about to turn away*.) Stay! here is one.   (*Hands letter*.   Rob *takes it eagerly, looks at it, and sighs*.)

*Rob.*   Are there no more?

*Rowell* (*sneeringly*).   No.   *She* does not seem inclined to write.

*Rob.*   I think *she* has written, not once, but many times.

*Rowell.*   Indeed!   'Tis strange you should never have received them, for our mails come very regular.

*Rob.*   Not so very strange, colonel.   We are in an enemy's country.   Craft and deceit are all about us, even in our own ranks.   I suspect an enemy has intercepted my letters.   I suspect you, colonel.

*Rowell* (*rising*).   Do you dare, Robert Trueworth?   Remember who I am. — one high in authority, your superior.   You are but a private soldier.   There is no love between us.   Be warned in time.

*Rob.*   Yes, I do remember; but I do not fear you. You have used your power to degrade me, by keeping me in the ranks, when I have *won* a higher place. I have not murmured.   But when you step between me and the girl I love, the girl I have won, mark me,

5*

colonel, *won* in spite of you, you are no longer my superior: you are a base and treacherous spy.

*Rowell* (*furious*). Robert Trueworth, you lie! you have not won her.

*Crimp* (*rises to a stooping position, throws off flag*). By golly! dere's gwine to be a fight here. Wish Massa Rob jes had dat letter. (*Creeps round to* L. *on " all fours" while the others are speaking.*)

*Rob.* In the sight of Heaven she is mine. We have exchanged vows; and, as I am true, I believe she is true. O man, man! have you no honor? Your strategy is unworthy a soldier of the Union. (GRANT *and* BOXER *cross stage* L. *to* R., *outside.*)

*Rowell.* I repeat, you have not won her. True, there was a foolish plighting of vows: but one year ago, when, as her guardian, I met her in Grainlow to surrender my trust, I found her changed. I felt she had repented of her rashness: now I am sure of it. She no longer loves you.

*Rob.* I will believe that when I hear it from her lips. You cannot shake my faith in her.

*Rowell* (*handing open letter*). Then read that. I am recalled to Grainlow.

*Rob* (*takes letter, and looks at it, then at* ROWELL, *then at letter*). "Come to Grainlow: I have repented of my rudeness to you — long to see you — earnestly entreat you to return — you shall be made happy." — oh! what is this? (*Crushes letter in his hand.*) She has forgotten me, repents. Oh! would I were dead!

*Crimp* (*aside*). Yaas, Guess not. What a muss! If he only had dat ar letter! (*Creeps nearer.*)

*Rowell.* There is only one construction to be placed upon that. 'Tis I who am the favored suitor. (GRANT *and* BOXER *saunter across stage outside from* R. *to* L. GRANT *appears at window, leans on the casing, and watches the scene, smoking;* BOXER *with him.*)

*Rob.* 'Tis false! more of your treachery. She would never have rejected me without a word, a sign.

*Rowell.* Still incredulous; poor fool! To your quarters! Another word to your superior, and you are under arrest. I have waited my time; and now Gaylie Gifford and her fortune shall be mine, in spite of trusting love and plighted vows. Away! (*Goes to* R.)

*Rob.* No: I will not stir. I know you have intercepted my letters; I know you have one in your bosom now; I saw you from my post secrete it; I saw the direction upon it; and by this (*showing letter*) I recognize the hand. 'Tis my property, and I claim it. Give it to me; or forgetting all distinctions, remembering only I am a man persecuted and wronged, I'll tear it from you.

*Rowell* (*taking pistol from his bosom*). Approach me but a step, and I'll have your life! I should be justified, for this is mutiny.

*Rob.* No, this is justice. I claim my rights. Give me the letter. (*Approaches.*)

*Rowell.* Take that instead! (*Raises arm.*)

*Crimp* (*running between, and throwing up his arm*). D-d-d-don't shoot! (*Pistol discharged.*) W-w-what you 'bout? w-want to blow dis yer darky's head off?

*Rowell* (*runs to door*). Guard, guard! Quick, quick! (*Guard has passed out of sight,* L.)

*Crimp* (*running to* Rob, *and falling on his knees at his side,* L.; *speaks quick*). Massa Rob, you's made a fo-fo ob yourself. Here's de letter right straight from Miss Gaylie. (*Passes letter into his hand.*)

*Rob.* Who are you?

*Crimp.* Done ye know me? I'se Crimp ob de Home-Guard. (Rowell *returns; guard enters door: should all be done quick.*)

*Rowell* (*to guard*). Arrest that man. To the guard-house with him!

*Rob* (*presses* Gaylie's *letter to his lips*). At last, at last! (*To* Rowell.) Ay! to the guard-house let it be. She has outwitted you. Here's a letter from her own dear hand.

*Rowell.* Ah! who has done this? Away with him! (*Guard places his hand on his shoulder.*) To the guard-house. (*Enter* Grant *door in* F., *writing on tablet in his hand.*)

*Grant.* Right. To the guard-house: orders must be obeyed. (*To* Rob.) If it comes to a trial, you may want a friend. (*Gives paper.*) Count on me.

*Rowell* (R.). And who are you?

*Grant* (*takes off hat*). Your superior, sir.

*Rowell* (*confused*). Gen. Grant? (*Salutes.*)

*Crimp.* By golly! it's de ole smoke-jack. Hi! whose pipe's out now?

*Tableau.* Gen. Grant c. Boxer *at door.* Rowell R., *saluting but confused.* Rob L. C., *saluting. Guard with his hand on his shoulder.* Crimp *on his knees* L., *squeezing himself, and laughing internally, with a show of white eyeballs and grinning teeth. Slow curtain.*

ACT III. — (*Two years later.*)  *Parlor in* GAYLIE GIF-
FORD'S *house.  Door in flat,* C., *windows each side
of it, with drapery curtains; shrubbery outside.
Table,* R. C., *with books, &c.; a lighted astral lamp
upon it.  Lounge,* L.  *Arm-chair,* R., *with small table
beside it.  Easy-chairs,* R. *and* L.  *Should be hand-
somely furnished; elegantly, if possible, by adding
statuettes, screens, &c.* MRS. TRUEWORTH *discovered
in arm-chair,* R., *knitting.* MATTIE *sitting at table,* L.
C., *reading a newspaper.*

*Mattie (dropping paper).*  And so at last this cruel
war is over, mother.  Richmond has fallen, and our
brave soldiers are already marching homeward.  Only
think of it! any day, any hour, may bring back our
dear Rob, after four years' absence.  Oh! 'twill be a
happy return for all of us.

*Mrs. T.*  For you and me, Mattie, yes.  I shall see
my brave boy again; you, a noble brother, whose record in the long struggle is spotless.  But how will
Gaylie receive him?

*Mattie.*  With open arms, mother: are they not
lovers?

*Mrs. T.*  They parted as lovers: but you know two
years ago Wilder Rowell resigned his command, and
returned to Grainlow; that from that time he has
been a constant visitor to this house; that he is always
welcomed by its mistress; that he attends her in all
her walks and drives; that she smiles upon him, and

evidently delights in his company. You know this, and I know it, and I don't like it. There, I've dropped a stitch!

*Mattie.* Why, mother! I really believe you are jealous of Col. Rowell's attentions. Do *you* doubt Gaylie's affection for us, her love for Brother Rob?

*Mrs. T.* Doubt her affection for us? No! Has she not been a dear daughter to me for these years? Has she not made us members of her own household? Have I not had, every day, convincing proofs of her affection? No, no! bless her dear heart, for Mother Trueworth has a warm corner in it. It's only for the boy I fear. Suppose he should come home, and find our Gaylie's heart turned from him, caught by this man whom I don't like, never did like, and never will like. There goes another stitch!

*Mattie.* Suppose, suppose! O mother, you ought to be ashamed of yourself! Why, I should no more doubt Gaylie's love for our Rob, than I should doubt—

*Mrs. T.* Your love for Hiram Jenks, eh, Mattie?

*Mattie.* There's another jealous one! He thinks Mr. Rowell is in love with me, or pretends he does, and continually quarrels with me about him. But we always make up, and I really believe that it's for the pleasure of being reconciled every day that he does it.

*Mrs. T.* Ah! Hiram Jenks is a good, honest, smart, reliable young man : so you be careful, and not quarrel too often. There may be a time when there will be no reconciliation.

*Mattie.* I'm not afraid of that, mother. He loves

me dearly. But I mean to cure him of this folly the very next time he attempts it.

*Crimp* (*outside*). Hi! whar's Missy Gaylie? whar she be? Hallelujum! (*Enters, c., running, in a high state of excitement.*) Babylum am fallen! Got a telegram down dar: de boys am coming dis yer night, got mos' home. Der a-lighting up down dar. "Johnny am marching home" double-quick. Yaas, indeed! Whar Miss Gaylie? Hi! lots ob fun.

*Mrs. T.* Coming, Crimp, to-night?

*Crimp.* Don't I tole you? Don't I tole you? I'se jes' gwine to 'luminate dis yer mamsum from de crown to de heel, regardless ob expense. Hi, golly! Jubilum am a-comun, and de darkies are jes' gwine into glory. Whar's Miss Gaylie? Whar she be? Golly! I can' hole myself still: mus' do somfum, or I shall combusticate and smash all to pieces. Whar's Miss Gaylie? (*Runs off*, L.)

*Mrs. T.* (*rising*). Coming to-night! Dear, dear boy! I must dress myself to receive him. Just see what a state I'm in, — this old cap and this poor dress.

*Mattie.* Why, mother, you never looked better in your life.

*Mrs. T.* It's no such thing. I'm looking shabby, and my boy's coming home. Oh! I wish I had the regal robes of a queen, that I might receive him as he deserves. Dear, dear boy! (*Hurries off*, L.)

*Mattie.* And so Rob is really coming home: how glad somebody will be to see him! She care for Wilder Rowell? I, for one, do not believe it. She's some reason for allowing his attentions: what it is, I cannot find out. When I ask her, she laughs, and breaks away singing, "Trust her not, she is fooling thee. Beware! Take care!" But I do trust her. She is all goodness. (*Enter* ROWELL, C.)

*Rowell* (*aside*). Ah! only pretty Mattie Trueworth. If I hadn't higher aspirations, I should dearly like to make love to that girl. (*Aloud*.) Good-evening, Miss Mattie.

*Mattie.* Ah! Mr. Rowell, good-evening.

*Rowell.* There seems to be a hubbub about this usually quiet mansion. What is going on?

*Mattie.* Why, don't you know our soldiers are coming home to-night?

*Rowell.* To-night! That is news. Is the war over?

*Mattie.* Why, what a man! Don't you read the papers? Don't you take any interest in the war?

*Rowell* (*aside*). Not since I resigned two years ago. (*Aloud*.) Oh, certainly! Is Richmond taken?

*Mattie.* A week ago. Here's the whole account. (*Rises with paper, and comes forward.*)

*Rowell.* Indeed! show it to me. (*Puts his arm about her waist.* HIRAM *appears at door*, C.)

*Hiram.* Ahem! a-hem! (MATTIE *starts to* L. ROWELL, *with paper in his hand, starts* R.)

*Hiram* (*with bombastic fury.*) Oh, yes, oh, yes! it is all true, all true.

*Rowell.* What! is the news confirmed?

*Hiram* (*contemptuously*). Confirmed! my *suspicions* are confirmed. (*To* MATTIE.) Oh, you cruel, deceitful, perfidious, ungenerous, ungrateful, unkind, unjust, un — un — unsociable young woman! what have you done?

*Rowell* (*aside*). Hallo! this fellow's in his jealous humor again. (*Aloud.*) Miss Mattie, as you have company, I'll take the paper, and find the news myself.

[*Exit* L.

*Mattie.* Mr. Hiram Jenks, what's the matter?

*Hiram.* What's the matter? You ask *me?* Matter, what's the mattie? I mean Wattie, matts the water? Oh, pshaw! I can't speak. My tongue is paralyzed. False woman! you have shattered the shrine of affection in this bosom. Young lady, you have burst the bonds of devotion. Young maiden, you have lacerated my heart, crushed my soul, blasted my hopes, destroyed my — my — Go, deceitful maid! After my long devotion, oh! this is too much, after all I have done for you. Oh! (*Tears hair.*)

*Mattie.* Well, what have you done for me?

*Hiram.* Eh! well, what I was going to do for you, — marry you. To see you fondly reclining upon the bosom of another, another's arm about your waist, — oh. this is torture! madness! (*Tears his hair, and rushes about stage.*) Mattie Trueworth, you are a cartless hoquette; no, a —

*Mattie.* You got the cart before the horse that time. Hiram. How silly you are! It's all a mistake.

*Hiram* (*coolly*). Oh! it's a mistake: I'm glad of that; so let's kiss and make up. (*Approaching her.*)

*Mattie.* Stop! you have opened my eyes. You saw his arm about my waist. Then he loves me. Oh, joy! rapture! bliss!

*Hiram.* Why, Mattie! you don't mean, you can't mean, you can't be so mean as to say you love Col. Rowell.

*Mattie.* Why not? he's rich; he is the owner of Trueworth Farm; and I, I might be again its mistress.

*Hiram.* Yes: but, Mattie, wh-wh-what's to become of me?

*Mattie.* You? why, you unjustly suspected me; but then you opened my eyes. You have my thanks: all else is at an end between us.

*Hiram.* Good gracious! I don't want your thanks. I wouldn't thank you for your thanks. I want *you*, Mattie. Come, let's make up (*coaxingly*). Now, do, Mattie. now, do. You ain't a-going to throw me over for that man?

*Mattie.* Why, he owns Trueworth Farm.

*Hiram* (*aside*). Confound it! she means it. (*Aloud.*) Hang Trueworth Farm! what's that to a heart filled with devotion! No, don't be hard on a feller. You know I love you. Come, let's make up. Do, now, do.

*Mattie* (*drawing herself up to her full length*). No, sir! You have trifled with me, and we must part. Seek another mate: be happy if you can. (*Imitating Hiram's coaxing.*) Do, now, do. I wish you well: particularly. *fare*-well. (*Courtesies, and goes off,* L.)

*Hiram* (*looks after her*). Why! she's gone. She means it! Jealous of her? why, it's absurd! She might have known it. I only wanted to tease her into a reconciliation: these make-ups are so jolly! But she don't tease well; and now I've set her to setting her cap for Rowell. Pshaw! Humbug! the jealous game is all up. (*Enter* CRIMP, L.)

*Crimp.* Hallo, Hi-*ram*! am dat you? Jes' you

come down to de barn wid me. I'll show you, free gratis, for nuffin, no extra charge, and no postfonemet, de greatest dissemblage ob sky — sky — sky — what dat man call 'em? *skyrotechnicks,* golly! rickets, fourteen pounders, and — and Rum-and-candles, and — and Bungola lights, and squabs, and bombs — golly! Jes' busters; de take de roof right off; yaas, indeed! Come down, do, Hi-*ram:* gwine to let 'em shoot slam bang, when de boys come home.

*Hiram.* That's right, Crimp: give them a welcome.

*Crimp.* Yaas, indeed, Hi-*ram!* gwine to make 'em smell brimstone. I tole you. Serve 'em right: wish we could get up a yearthquake: wouldn't be a bit too good for 'em. Come on, Hi. I say, Hi-*ram,* am you any relation to ole Jim? he was de highest old ram eber I see. Yah, yah, yah! (*Exit,* c., *laughing, followed by* HIRAM. *Enter from* L., ROWELL.)

*Rowell.* And so the war is over, and the boys are marching home, and with them comes, of course, Mr. Rob Trueworth. Hang the luck! I fear that fellow's appearance. Two years ago I resigned my command in the army for two reasons. First, an unfortunate *rencontre* with Trueworth, whom I kept in the ranks after he had been several times honorably mentioned, awakened the suspicions of Grant, and a court-martial was threatened; second, a very pressing invitation from Gaylie to return, the pretext being business which required my assistance, but the real motive, an evident desire for my society. Of the first reason, I took good care to let her know nothing; and having the post-master, Hosea Jenks, well under my thumb, I am sure she has received no hint from Trueworth. She has evidently repented of her folly, and takes kindly to my presence. Never a word about Rob Trueworth. Yet I seem no nearer the attainment of my heart's desire, than when I returned. I have assiduously courted her: we walk, ride, and sail together. I am attentive, devoted, and she enjoys every thing. But, when I speak of love, she evades it, or talks of her freedom, or we are interrupted. I will speak plainly: she must be bound to me ere he returns, or I fear my two-years' campaign will be wasted. Ah! here she is. (*Enter* GAYLIE. L.)

*Gaylie.* Oh, isn't it glorious! the war is over. (*Sees* ROWELL.) Why, colonel, is that you? Have you been waiting long? I'm so sorry.

*Rowell* (*taking her hand*). Yes: I have been waiting long, two years, Gaylie, to give you full assurance that I love you. Is my love returned?

*Gaylie* (*excitedly*). Returned! O colonel! have you heard the news? Our brave soldiers have returned; that is, they are coming home to-night, crowned with victory. Oh, I'm so happy! ain't you?

*Rowell.* Gaylie, I am miserable.

*Gaylie.* Because they are coming home? Oh, fie! colonel. And you a soldier?

*Rowell.* Gaylie, you must listen to me. You evade a question of the utmost importance to my welfare. I asked you, Do you love me?

*Gaylie.* As you have asked me a dozen times in the last fortnight; and I answer you as I have before, Wait until the war is over.

*Rowell.* Ah, but the war is over: there is no reason for delay. Gaylie, will you be my wife?

*Gaylie.* That's a serious question, colonel. I'll consider it.

*Rowell.* Gaylie, you'll drive me mad.

*Gaylie.* Then I won't consider it: will that suit you? O colonel! do you suppose there have been any changes in the regiment?

*Rowell.* Will you answer my question, Gaylie?

*Gaylie.* Will you answer mine, colonel?

*Rowell* (*biting his lips*). I don't know; I don't care. Boxer, who took my place, has been made a brigadier-general; but, for the rest, I know nothing.

*Gaylie.* I wonder if Rob Trueworth is still a private. Perhaps he's a captain, or a sergeant. I do hope he has risen.

*Rowell.* You still have an interest in that fellow?

*Gaylie.* Of course. Isn't he my brother?

*Rowell* (*aside*). That's good. She ignores the other tie. (*Aloud.*) Now, Gaylie, speak. (*Takes her hand.*) Surely my devotion deserves a recompense. Will you? (*Enter* CRIMP, L., *with a lighted candle in each hand.*)

*Crimp* (*speaking as he enters*). Hi! Miss Gaylie, de hole *circumbendence* ob de exterior ob de house up stairs am in a blaze ob glory; lights into all de windows, an' greeze all ober de glass and de carpets. Took sum pains up dar, I tole you. Shall I light dese yer windows, Miss Gaylie?

*Gaylie.* No, Crimp, I will attend to this.

*Crimp.* Yaas, indeed! I'm obleeged to you. Jes' put your bright eyes into de windows, and de illumination up stairs won't be no circumstance. I'll jes' stick 'em into de bay window, out yunder. [*Exit* R.

*Rowell* (*runs to Gaylie, and puts his arm about her waist; takes her hand*). Gaylie, am I never to get an answer? Speak before we are again interrupted. (MRS. TRUEWORTH *appears*, L.)

*Rowell* (*goes* L.). Confusion! Will this never end?

*Gaylie.* Come in, mother.

*Mrs. T.* No: when two young people are so closely interested in conversation, an old woman's presence is unpleasant. I'm not blind, Gaylie Gifford; and I'm not likely to hold my tongue, when I see injustice done one I love: so I'll go away. O Gaylie! Gaylie! have I been deceived in you? (*Going.*)

*Gaylie* (*running to her*). No, mother, no! Believe me, trust me.

*Mrs. T.* I try to, Gaylie; but it is so hard, so hard! [*Exit* L.

*Gaylie* (*comes down* R. *at table*). Have I wounded her dear heart? Am I doing right?

*Rowell* (*approaching*). Gaylie —

*Gaylie.* Silence, sir! Speak to me now, and I shall hate you. (ROWELL *returns* L. *Enter* C. HOSEA JENKS, *followed by* HIRAM. MATTIE *enters* L. HOSEA *comes down.* HIRAM *stops up stage, and tries to make up with* MATTIE; *she snubs him.*)

*Hosea.* I — I — really, really, I beg pardon, colonel, if you are having a *tety-tety;* but I thought you'd like your mail, and so I brought it. (*Comes down* L. *of table, and hands letters to* ROWELL, *who stands* R. *of table; then goes back to* L. C.)

*Rowell.* Ah! thank you, Jenks. (*Aside.*) Confound his kindness! I know you'll excuse me, Gaylie. Here's my mail.

*Gaylie.* Certainly, colonel. (HIRAM *comes down* R. *of table, where* GAYLIE *is standing, and hands her a letter secretly.*) (*Aside.*) And here's mine. (*Presses it to her lips.*)

*Rowell* (*his back to* GAYLIE). (*Aside.*) Here's one for Gaylie, in the old familiar hand. (*Looks round to her: she is looking down; he turns to* L., *and slips it into his pocket; as he does so, she bends forward, and watches him, then shakes her head.*)

*Gaylie.* Nothing for me, Mr. Jenks? (*She looks at* JENKS *keenly: he tries to look in her face, drops his eyes, and nervously plays with his hat.*)

*Hosea.* Oh, no! Nothing for you, not a thing. Do you suppose I should have failed to bring them? (*She goes up stage; he comes down* R.) (*Aside.*) That's a lie, a wicked lie. I can't help it. I try; but it will pop out, anywhere, everywhere. Once I was a punster. "Alas, poor Jenks! where are your jests now, that were wont to set the table in a roar?" All lies now.

*Gaylie* (*goes up, takes* HIRAM's *hand*). (*Aside.*) Thanks, faithful sentinel. (*Aloud.*) Come, Mattie, we'll go and look at Crimp's preparations, and leave the colonel to his letters. (*Puts her arm about* MATTIE's *waist, and they go off* C.)

*Rowell* (*who has opened a letter, and is reading it, seated at table,* L.). Confound it! another call for money, and no way to raise it. (JENKS *starts for door;*

Rowell *looks round*.)   Yes; there's Jenks: he must help me out.   Jenks!

*Hosea* (*turns trembling*).   Ye-yes, colonel.

*Rowell* (*rising*).   Jenks, I must have money at once. I have a pressing call, and my funds are completely exhausted.   Come, you shall give me fifteen hundred dollars, and I'll transfer to you the Trueworth Farm.

*Hosea* (*aside*).   That's cool.   (*Aloud.*)   But — but you see, colonel, I — I — I don't want the Trueworth Farm.

*Col.*   Neither do I.   But I do want money; so look round and raise it, and don't keep me waiting long (*rises, and comes close to him*), or Grainlow will have a new postmaster.   (*Exit* c.   JENKS *falls into chair he has left.*)

*Hosea.*   New p-p-p-postmaster!   well, that's the old threat.   Oh, the villain!   This comes of meddling with public affairs.   When I was a private citizen, I was gay and happy, with such a flow of humor, punning from morning till night.   I never pun now: I can't; it's sure to turn into a lie.   I'm a miserable old rascal, that's ashamed to look an honest man in the face.. I'm a swindler, a cheat, a liar, and a coward.   I can't help it. I sold my birthright for a mess of pottage; no, potash, for it's all lie.   O Jenks! when you parted with honesty, you knocked down a rich estate at an awful sacrifice.   I'm in daily dread of these infernal detectives. In my office, at home, at my table, in bed, I feel the hand of justice on my shoulder, and the voice of outraged Uncle Sam thunders in my ear.

*Hiram.*   The colonel wants his money, dad.

*Hosea (starts to his feet).* Yes, yes. I'm a-going for it, I'm a-going for it. (*Starts up stage.*)

*Hiram.* Halt! 'bout face! hold up your head, turn out your toes. (HOSEA *obeys.*) Now, dad, you will do no such thing!

*Hosea.* Hey! what do you mean, boy?

*Hiram.* Come, dad, straighten up; drop that. I've changed that name with you. You are the boy, — a weak, silly, foolish boy.

*Hosea.* Do you want to insult my gray hairs?

*Hiram.* Insult them? Tell me, dad, have *you* respected them as you should?

*Hosea.* Eh! wh-what do you mean?

*Hiram.* Why does that man order you to find money for him? Why does he treat you with such cool contempt?

*Hosea (nervously).* Eh? oh! ha, ha, ha! it's only his way, you know. We are great friends, — great friends. He got me my office; and, you know, if I can do him a favor, why, I ought; certainly I oughter be proud to — to do him a favor: see? (*Aside.*) How he looks at me! he knows it's a lie. I can't help it: it will pop out.

*Hiram.* That won't do, dad. You're afraid of him: you're a coward.

*Hosea.* Coward, boy! this to me?

*Hiram.* Yes, and more. You have sold yourself to this man; you are accomplices in crime. You have made yourself liable to a long imprisonment, for you have robbed the mail.

*Hosea (alarmed).* Hush! don't speak so loud, boy!

Who told you this?  Do you want to see me hung? do
you want— O Hiram, Hiram! pity me, pity me!
I'm a poor old sinner, a poor old sinner!  (*Wrings his
hands, falls on his knees, and hides his face.*)

*Hiram.*   That's the truth, dad; a tool in the hands
of a crafty man.  O dad, you were hard on me in
the old days!  You sought to crush out my ambition to
be manly while yet a boy, — an ambition which should
have been encouraged, not crushed.  Your example
made others slight me, and look upon me as a fool.
But you were an honest man, and you made me honest; and for that I shall always be grateful.  Now you
have parted with your high estate; sold yourself, body
and soul, to the — well, Col. Rowell is his name.  I
have kept mine, and I mean to rescue you from the
clutches of this villain.

*Hosea.*   No, boy, you can't do that; I'm sold, delivered: it's too late.  I see my folly.  But that man!
O Hiram! he could deliver me up to justice: he could
have me imprisoned.

*Hiram.*   Why, dad, you forget he is your confed-
erate; that, in sacrificing you, he must betray himself.

*Hosea.*   Eh? I never thought of that.  Of course he
must.  What a fool I have been!  He dare not move.
I'm safe, I'm safe!

*Hiram.*   But I dare, dad, and I will.  For four
years you have intercepted letters belonging to Gaylie,
and Rob Trueworth.  I know it: I have full proof.
Ah! I've watched you closer than you watched me
when I was a boy.

*Hosea.*   Yes, yes: but you can't betray me; you

couldn't have the heart. Hiram, I was a good father to you; that is, I tried to be. You won't give me up to justice?

*Hiram.* You have wronged my friends. Unless you immediately resign your office, I will give information that shall lead to your arrest.

*Hosea.* I'll resign, I'll resign! but he won't let me.

*Hiram.* He shall not prevent you. You must also decline to furnish him with money.

*Hosea.* I'll do that, I'll do that!—any thing you ask, Hiram, only don't give me up.

*Hiram.* He's coming back. Remember, no money to that man. (*Goes up* R. *Enter* ROWELL, C.)

*Rowell.* Why, Jenks, what are you about? Didn't you hear? I want that money to-night,—must have it. Why are you not after it?

*Jenks.* You want fifteen hundred dollars, colonel?

*Rowell.* That's the sum I named.

*Jenks* (*comes close to him*). Don't you wish you may get it, colonel? (*Snaps his fingers in his face.*) Do you understand that? not a dollar from me. You've been drawing heavily on my conscience, but you can't draw on my bank-account: understand that.

*Rowell.* Fool! do you know that I could hang you, unless—

*Hosea.* We hang together. That's good, a pun, ha, ha, ha! the first for many a day. Oh, I'm feeling decidedly better! No, colonel, you couldn't hang me: you dare not molest me; for we are both in the same boat.

*Rowell.* Indeed! Well, my *honest* friend, we can find a new postmaster for Grainlow.

*Hosea.* Do, colonel! the sooner you write to Washington, "Off with his head: so much for Jenks," the better for said Jenks.

*Rowell.* Do you refuse to purchase the Trueworth Farm?

*Hosea.* Decidedly I do.

*Hiram (comes down).* Do I understand you, colonel? You wish to dispose of Trueworth Farm?

*Rowell.* What's that to you?

*Hiram.* If you want to sell, I'm your customer.

*Rowell.* You?

*Hosea.* You? Why, Hiram Jenks, where can you find the money?

*Hiram.* No matter, dad. Name your price, colonel.

*Rowell.* Fifteen hundred dollars.

*Hiram (takes a wallet from his pocket, and slaps it on table).* There's your money.

*Hosea.* The boy's crazy. *(Aside to H.)* I say, Hiram, what are you about? You wouldn't let me buy it, and now —

*Hiram.* I want it: you forget you are under suspicion. Uncle Sam might confiscate your property at any moment, and the farm would go with it.

*Hosea.* Oh, what a head, what a head! And I thought him a boy!

*Hiram.* If you want the money to-night, write a receipt, and take it. We will pass the papers in the morning.

*Rowell (goes to table, R., and writes).* Certainly.

*Hiram* (*takes paper from his pocket*). As I have had some thoughts of making you an offer for the property, I have drawn up an agreement. Sign that, and I am satisfied.

*Rowell* (*takes paper, and looks at it*). This is satisfactory. (*Signs.*)

*Hiram.* Now, dad, if you will witness it. (*Takes bills from wallet.*)

*Hosea.* Certainly. (*Signs. Aside.*) Where could that boy have got his money?

*Hiram* (*taking paper, and laying down bills*). You'll find that all right.

*Rowell* (*counting money*). All correct. I will see you at Lawyer Ware's office, to-morrow at nine. Is that satisfactory?

*Hiram.* Perfectly. Come, dad, let's look after the office.

*Hosea.* Yes, to the office, where I shall take the first opportunity to write to the Postmaster General, resigning my office.

*Rowell.* Do it at your peril!

*Hosea.* No: I shall do it at my office. Ha, ha, ha! Why, I'm getting back into my old humor, thanks to the boy. What a head! I used to look in his face, and think I saw a fool. I was wrong: I should have looked in a glass.

*Rowell.* I hope the farm will pay you better than it has me, Hiram.

*Hiram.* No doubt it will. (*Aside.*) If Miss Mattie Trueworth wants Trueworth Farm, she'll have to look this way. Come, dad!

7

*Hosea.* Good-by, colonel: if you want your next mail, you'll have to come for it. (HIRAM *goes up, followed by* HOSEA; *meet* GAYLIE *and* MATTIE *coming in;* MATTIE *comes down* R., *is stopped by* HIRAM; GAYLIE *speaks with* HOSEA, L. C.)

*Hiram.* Mattie, won't you make up?

*Mattie.* No, sir: I have higher aspirations.

*Hiram* (*tragically*). I know: to the owner of Trueworth Farm! Mattie, it's hard to lose you, but it's for the best: I see my error. I cannot win you; and so I freely give you up to a better, a richer man, — the owner of Trueworth Farm. Farewell! (*Clasps her in his arms quick, and kisses her: she screams; he runs off* C.)

*Mattie.* Well, I never! what does he mean? He give me up? He shall do no such thing. Dear, dear! have I lost him? Hiram, Hiram! (*Runs off* C.)

*Gaylie.* Your son has gone, Mr. Jenks.

*Hosea.* Has he? I must run after him. I can't bear to have him out of my sight: I'm so proud of him! (*Aside.*) He might repent, and give me up.

[*Exit* C.

*Rowell* (*as* GAYLIE *comes down*). Gaylie, may I ask a favor of you? I have been making a sale to-night, and have here fifteen hundred dollars: will you give me your check for it? I want to send it to-night.

*Gaylie.* Certainly! you'll find my check-book in the next room. Please bring it to me, colonel. (ROWELL *bows, and exits* L.; GAYLIE *sits in chair* R., *and looks after him.*) That man loves me, for two years has been my devoted slave; and now the time has come for me to speak plainly. He tells me there is no

longer reason for delay: he is right.  He thinks his
long period of devotion deserves a recompense: he
shall have it.  And the other, Rob Trueworth, who
left here four years ago, — does he still love me?
(*Smiles.*)  Can I doubt it?  Yet I must speak to-night,
speak plainly.  He believes that he has won me: I can
see it in his proud step, the triumphant glance of his
eye.  Is he right? (*Smiles.*)   Can I doubt that?
(*Enter* ROWELL L., *with check-book.*)   I'm so sorry to
trouble you, colonel! (*Takes book.*)  Fifteen hundred,
you say? (*Writes check.*)

*Rowell* (*laying down bills*).  Yes: you'll find the
bills here.

*Gaylie.*   So you have made a sale to-night, colonel?

*Rowell.*   Yes: Trueworth Farm.

*Gaylie.*   Sold Trueworth Farm?  And you refused
to sell it to me four years ago!

*Rowell.*   Yes, — yes, I remember.  I didn't like to
part with it now, but I wanted money —

*Gaylie* (*rising*).  Oh! I bear you no malice, colonel.  (*Gives check.*)

*Rowell.*  Thank you.  And now, Gaylie, that we
are alone, may I once more press you for an answer?
(*Takes her hand, and puts his arm about her waist.*)
You know how dearly I love you: make me happy by
saying that you return that love.

*Gaylie.*   And would that really make you happy,
colonel?

*Rowell.*   Happy?  The happiest of men!

*Gaylie* (*drawing herself up*).  Then hear me, Col.
Rowell! (*Enter* L. MRS. TRUEWORTH, *with shawl and*

*bonnet added to her former costume, and a large band-box in her hand.*)

*Rowell.* Oh, speak, Gaylie! tell me you love me!

*Mrs. T.* Before you do, Gaylie, let me get out of this house. (GAYLIE *goes* R., ROWELL L.)

*Gaylie.* Mother, what does this mean?

*Mrs. T.* Mother! you have no right to call me by that name: you have disgraced it. Four years ago you plighted vows with my dear boy; he went to battle, trusting in your promise: and now another's arms are about you, another's voice pleading to you for words which tremble on your lips. O Gaylie! how I have loved you, you may never know; but I love my boy, and he shall not come here to have his noble heart broken at the sight of his rival, a favored suitor. No: I thank you for all your kindness to me, but — my boy's coming, and I'll go to meet him: he has no one to love him now so tenderly as his old mother, bless him! 'Twill be a hard blow after all his love and hope and faith. O Gaylie, Gaylie! you've broken my heart! (*Drops her box, and staggers forward; GAYLIE runs, and catches her in her arms.*)

*Gaylie.* O mother, mother! this must not be! Stay here; this is your home: here Rob will come —

*Mrs. T.* Not in that man's presence will I meet my boy.

*Rowell* (*aside*). The old lady's complimentary. (*Aloud.*) I think Mrs. Trueworth is right, Gaylie. It would certainly be unpleasant to young Trueworth to see our happiness.

*Gaylie.* I beg your pardon, colonel: I have not spoken yet.

*Mrs. T.* Let me go, Gaylie: I cannot stay here!

*Gaylie.* You must, you shall, mother! You have heard the colonel: now hear me.

*Mrs. T.* No, no! I will go. Hark! what's that? (*Distant chorus; sings the chorus of "Marching through Georgia."*)

*Gaylie.* At last, at last! They've come, mother, they've come. Hear me. Within myself, and to myself, I made a vow that I would keep Col. Rowell in suspense until I heard the victorious shouts of our returning heroes. They come, and I can speak; hear me: Col. Rowell, you have asked me to be your wife: I answer, No; for I detest you. (MRS. TRUEWORTH *goes over to chair*, R.)

*Rowell.* Gaylie, what is this? are you in earnest?

*Gaylie.* Four years ago I defied you; enlisted, for the war between you and my hero, on his side, not yours. I have kept the faith: I have battled you from that time to this, and won the victory.

*Rowell.* Battled! victory! I do not understand you.

*Gaylie.* You sought to keep us apart, and, to that end, intercepted our letters.

*Rowell.* No, no! you are mistaken! I — I am innocent of any such crime. (*Enter* HIRAM, R.)

*Gaylie.* Here is my witness. 'Twas he who aided me in outwitting you. For the last two years our letters have passed under cover of his name. Those you have stopped were decoys.

*Rowell* (*aside*). What a fool I have been!

*Gaylie.* You sought to keep my hero in the ranks. Perhaps you will recollect the first letter which reached

7*

him. 'Twas sent by the hands of a trusty messenger. (*Enter* CRIMP, L.) 'Twas delivered in your presence.

*Crimp.* Yaas, colonel; d-d-don't shoot!

*Rowell* (*aside*). Oh, curse the girl! she has out-witted me.

*Gaylie.* You sought to keep him down; and so I decoyed you here, believing that your presence, hateful as it had become, was necessary to the exaltation of Rob Trueworth. I have used a woman's art, coquetry; but the end justifies the means. So you see, colonel, the Home Guard has a right to claim the victory. Home Guard, attention! fall in! (*She stands* L. HIRAM *takes his place next her, and* CRIMP *next up stage.* GAYLIE *then faces them.*)

*Gaylie.* Comrades, your general, ahem! is proud of you; we have fought together; we have conquered. Now let us march to meet the returning heroes. (*Steps back beside* HIRAM.) Home Guard, attention! Eyes right! eyes left! Salute! (*They salute. Chorus repeated outside, "Marching through Georgia," nearer. Enter* ROB, *in full uniform of a colonel.*) Ah! Rob, Rob! he's come, mother, he's come! (*Runs into* ROB's *arms.*)

*Mrs. T.* (*springing up*). O Rob, boy! welcome, welcome, welcome!

*Rob.* Dear, dear mother! (*Enter* MATTIE, L.)

*Mattie.* Where is he? O Brother Rob! (*Runs into his arms.*) This is glorious!

*Rob.* Thanks for your hearty welcome. Ah, Hiram! (*Shakes hands.*) And Crimp!

*Crimp.* Yaas, indeed! how is yer? an' how is

Boxer? an'—an' ole smoke-jack? Gay times in ole Virginny, two years ago. I'm obleeged to you.

*Rob (comes down to* L., *where* ROWELL *stands with his back to him, and his arms folded*). Wilder Rowell, the regiment with which you set out for the battle-field has returned under command of its new colonel, myself.

*Rowell (turns round).* You the colonel of the 10th?

*Rob.* I am happy to say I have won that distinction. Won it! do you hear? You would have kept me in the ranks; but thanks to woman's wit, and military justice, you were removed in time. I now return to claim my bride. (*Turns up stage.*)

*Rowell (turns away).* Oh, I have failed,—miserably failed! I cannot bear to see their happiness. (*All are gathered about* ROB, *up stage.*) I was so sure of her! and she has been laughing at me all this time. I wish I could hate her; but no, no, it's impossible. I played for her fortune, and I ended in loving her as I can never love again. They are busy: I'll slip away. Oh! this may be justice for them: 'tis ruin, utter ruin, for me. [*Exit* L.

*Hiram (leads* MATTIE *down* R.) Now, Mattie, Rob has returned, and Gaylie is true to him. Col. Rowell, of course, is in the market.

*Mattie.* I don't care if he is: I don't want him!

*Hiram.* But you want Trueworth Farm.

*Mattie.* Not if I must take it's owner.

*Hiram.* No? not when his name is Hiram Jenks? It's mine, Mattie: I bought it to-night. Come, let's kiss and make up: do, now, do! (*Kiss and retire up, arm in arm.* ROB *and* GAYLIE *come down.*)

*Rob.* Gaylie, how can I ever thank you for making me what I am?

*Gaylie.* Nonsense, Rob! you made yourself. If I did help a little, 'twas for my own pride; for I always wanted to be a colonel's wife. Ahem!

*Crimp* (*down* L.). So did I. Yaas, yaas! I'm obleeged to you. No, no, dat's a bifstake: dat's a bifstake. I mean — I mean — wh-w-w-what do I mean? I mean to go an' let off dem ar squabs; make a blaze; cos de colonel's come; yaas, indeed!

*Hiram* (R.) Wait, Crimp: the colonel's going to speak.

*Crimp.* Yaas, indeed! I's waiting with both years wide open tight. I'm obleeged to you.

*Rob* (C. *with* GAYLIE). Ladies and gentlemen of the Home Guard, accept my thanks for your kind and valuable assistance in the campaign just closed. Ever grateful must our country's defenders be to the strong arms and tender hands, loving hearts and watchful eyes, that cared for the old folks at home, when they were in the field.

*Gaylie* (C.). Ahem! Colonel, in behalf of the Home Guard, I give you a hearty welcome home. If our efforts have won your approbation, if— There, I've broken down! O Rob, Rob! I'm so glad to get you back! we'll be a happy family now, won't we, mother?

*Mrs. T.* (*comes down* R. C.). Indeed we will, Gaylie. My own boy back again, thank Heaven! The skies will be bright now.

*Rob.* Ay, mother! bright to herald the coming of peace, with all its blessings. We have fought the good fight: we have conquered.  Henceforth the land we love is free.

*Crimp.*  Das a fac', an' I am one on 'em; I'm obleeged to you.

*Gaylie.*  Yes, we have conquered; and, though " the girl you left behind you " has done but little for the cause, she carried into it a loyal and a willing heart; and, if her hero is satisfied, she will never regret having " enlisted for the war."

HIRAM *and* MATTIE, R.  MRS. T., ROB, GAYLIE, C. CRIMP, L.  *Curtain.*

# NEVER SAY DIE.

# NEVER SAY DIE.

## CHARACTERS.

Mr. Simon Graylock.
Mr. Ralph Cheeny.
John Bounce, Mr. Graylock's coachman
Mrs. Graylock.
Miss Alice Chase.
Patty Pert, Mrs. Graylock's maid.

COSTUMES MODERN AND APPROPRIATE.

Scene. — *Handsome apartment in the house of* Mr.
Graylock. *Table,* c., *red cloth. A study-lamp
burning. Books and papers. Lounge,* r. *Arm-
chair,* l. *Chairs* r. *and* l. *of table.* Patty Pert
*seated in arm-chair with a book.*

*Patty (reading).* "At the sound of that voice mu-
sically voluminous as the sighing of the October gale
in the lofty branches of mountain hemlocks, Araminta
Augusta Violetta sprang to her feet, and, dashing the
embroidery-frame to the floor with a crash that shook
the ancient edifice, gave one terrific, yet ecstatic scream

8                                                        85

of joy, and sank fainting into the arms of her own
fond Felix Frederick Freelove." Oh! isn't that splendid? Oh! why wasn't I born in those barbaric days,
when knights and squires, and milk-white steeds, and
high-born ladies, pranced about, like the grand entry of
a magnificent circus? Oh! why wasn't I a barbarian?
And such love-making! (*Reads.*) "Beauteous dam-
sel, with eyes of azure blue, hear, oh, hear the vow of
your own true knight! I will cleave yonder mountain
from summit to base with one blow of my trusty cime-
ter, ere one tear of grief shall find its way adown thy
gently-arching nose:" oh, beautiful, beautiful! There
are no barons now. Who ever hears such language
as that in these plebeian times? Even old Mr. Graylock, fond as he is of his young wife, never allows his
ecstasy to rise above the utterance of "My dear, you're
looking well, remarkably well." And Mrs. Graylock
has nothing more romantic on the end of her tongue
than, "Hubby, don't be gone long. I do get so sleepy
when you're away!" Oh, the world's degenerating!
there's not the least doubt of it. There's John Bounce,
who tries to make love to me; and precious bad business he makes of it too, forever dropping his *h*'s, and
sticking them where they don't belong. I'm determined
to reform him, or he shall bounce about the world without a wife, though, as he says, his 'art *h*is given to me
*h*alone. (*Enter* BOUNCE R.)

*Bounce.* 'Illo, Patty! *h*all by yourself, 'ay? Where's
the master and missus?

*Patty.* Still at table, Mr. Bounce, daintily toying
with the dessert of their luxurious repast.

*Bounce.* My *h*eyes, Patty! what *h*elegance of *h*expression!

*Patty.* It's a pity, Mr. Bounce, your language is not better seasoned with polite pronunciation.

*Bounce.* My *h*eyes, Patty, 'ave you been drinking?

*Patty.* Sir!

*Bounce.* You talk just for *h*all the world like the fellows that master used to 'ave 'ere to dine afore 'e was 'itched to the new missus. They were dreadful free *h*and *h*easy spoken until the wine came *h*on, and then they couldn't find words *h*expansive enough to *h*express their *h*ideas.

*Patty.* Mr. Bounce, no more of such language. It is time that you and I understood each other. I believe you wish me, at some not very distant period, to become your bride?

*Bounce.* Yes: *h*i *h*expect to make you Mrs. Bounce.

*Patty.* *H*expect? Why should you?

*Bounce.* Why, Patty? 'Aven't *h*i *h*offered you my 'art *h*and 'and?

*Patty.* And — and what?

*Bounce.* My 'art *h*and 'and. Don't you *h*understand *h*it?

*Patty.* Your art? Yes: your art is driving horses.

*Bounce.* But I ain't talking *h*about 'orses. *H*i said 'art; this 'art which 'eaves *h*in my bosom with fond *h*aspiration.

*Patty.* Nonsense! Once for all, Mr. John Bounce, I will never marry a man who aspirates in such a shocking manner as you do. No, sir. The man whose

bride I shall become must be capable of declaring his
love in grammatical, pronounceably correct English.
He must fall gracefully upon his knees before me, and,
in accents too wild to be resisted, say, "Patty, my
heart"—not *art*, Mr. Bounce; I'll have no artful man
—"is at your feet." Not *hat*. Hats are for heads,
not feet, Mr. Bounce. When you can do that, speak:
till then a gulf as wide as that which once yawned
between Felix Frederick Freelove, and his Araminta
Augusta Violetta, separates us.            [*Exit* R.

*Bounce.* My *h*eyes! Who's *H*aráminta *H*augusta?
*H*i don't know 'er. Well, this *h*is *h*extraordinary.
*H*and *h*i thought my language was so *h*intelligent!
Well, Miss Patty, though *h*i love you with *h*all my 'art,
*h*i'm not *h*a-going to lose no flesh on your *h*account.
Well, *h*after *h*all, women *h*are a good deal like 'orses;
*h*if they find you don't notice their capers, but keep
cool, they're very *h*apt to settle down *h*into a *h*easy
trot. 'Ere's master and missus. *H*i'll make myself
scarce. (*Exit* L. *Enter*, R., MR. GRAYLOCK, *with a
plate containing nuts and raisins balanced on each hand,
followed by* MRS. GRAYLOCK.)

*Mr. G.* Now, my dear, for a refreshing season of
calm and tranquil delight. Here, beneath our own
vine and fig-tree, metaphorically speaking, we will
meditate, converse, and—and eat our nuts and raisins. (*Sits in chair* L. *of table*).

*Mrs. G.* (*placing ottoman beside him,* L.). Yes, indeed; what could be more delightful? (*Sits. He
hands her a plate. They eat.*) How grateful I should
be—and I am—that I have a dear husband, so fond

of spending his evenings with me, instead of leaving me for a stupid club, or the society of a billiard-room! It's a shame, a disgrace to married life, the manner in which some husbands conduct themselves.

*Mr. G.* Ah, my dear, you were a wise young woman, when from the multitude of your admirers, young, giddy fellows, you turned to make choice of a staid, middle-aged, experienced individual to guide your youthful steps. Ah, my dear, yours was a wise choice. Do I not worship you? Do I not dote upon you? Is not every wish of your heart gratified?

*Mrs. G.* Yes, indeed. No: there's one wish yet ungratified. Alice —

*Mr. G.* What! you're not going to bring up that troublesome subject again?

*Mrs. G.* Again and again, until you give your consent to her marriage with Mr. Cheeny.

*Mr. G.* Now, my dear, how are we to enjoy a season of calm and tranquil delight if you insist upon boring me with a subject upon which we can never agree? Let's change the subject. My dear, I am seriously thinking of dyeing —

*Mrs. G.* O Simon, don't talk so! Do you want to frighten me to death?

*Mr. G.* Yes, of dyeing — my hair and beard.

*Mrs. G.* You cannot mean it.

*Mr. G.* Yes, I do. Watkins tells me he has a wonderful preparation, one application of which will instantly turn white, gray, red, or yellow hair to a beautiful black. Think of it, Susannah! In imagination behold your husband entering the room, trans-

6*

formed by " The Magic Dyer " into a youthful specimen of the genus *homo.*

*Mrs. G.* I couldn't imagine it, and I won't. I am perfectly satisfied with your appearance. And you would look horrid with your hair and beard in mourning. I should never forgive you if you did such a dreadful thing. Never say dye to me again. Now let's change that subject. Alice and Mr. Cheeny —

*Mr. G.* Sue! Susan! Susannah! pause. If you do not instantly pause, I shall dye — my hair and beard.

*Mrs. G.* Oh, no, you won't! Why are you so determined to keep Alice single? (*Enter* ALICE R.)

*Alice.* Yes, uncle, why am I to be deprived of my natural rights?

*Mr. G.* Oh, bother! You here? Now, how is a man to enjoy a season of —

*Mrs. G.* Oh, don't say that again! Answer my question.

*Mr. G.* Certainly, my dear. I have three reasons : the first of which is, she is too young to marry.

*Mrs. G. and Alice* (*together*). Too young to marry!

*Mr. G.* (*aside*). Grand chorus of indignant females. (*Aloud.*) I repeat it : too young to marry.

*Mrs. G.* Nonsense! She's as old as I am. If that is your opinion, why did you allow me to marry?

*Mr. G.* (*aside*). Stuck my foot in it. (*Aloud.*) You didn't allow me to finish. Too young to marry a young man.

*Alice.* Indeed! Well, I'll never marry an old one,

if I live to be as old as my grandmother. I do detest old men, and middle-aged men too.

*Mr. G.* (*aside*). Stuck my foot in it again.

*Mrs. G.* So much for your first reason. What is your second?

*Mr. G.* My second is, Alice can do better than to marry at all. Look at that head. How beautifully the reasoning bumps are developed! A phrenologist would go wild with ecstasy with his hands upon that head.

*Alice.* Would he? He'd get them well scratched for his assurance.

*Mr. G.* (*Rising, placing plate on table, and speaking with bombastic enthusiasm.*) Alice, 'tis the era of progress. Woman's rights will soon be fully recognized, and woman take her place among the gifted and the learned. They will be called to the bar, the pulpit. Think of that time, and prepare to take your place, — to rule, and not be ruled. Married life for you! Preposterous! 'Twould be a galling chain 'gainst which your noble intellect would chafe and worry.

*Alice.* Uncle, are you crazy?

*Mrs. G.* Poor Simon, has second childhood come so soon to you?

*Mr. G.* My dear, let's change the subject.

*Mrs. G.* Certainly; to the third and last reason. What is that?

*Mr. G.* The third and last? That I refuse to make public.

*Mrs. G.* What! you have another reason?

*Mr. G.* I have, and it's a clincher; but I positively refuse to give it.

*Mrs. G.*   To your own lawful wife? to her from whom you have often said you have no secrets? Simon Graylock, I'm ashamed of you.

*Mr. G.*   But, my dear Susan —

*Mrs. G.*   Don't dear me, Mr. Graylock. You are a very ungrateful man. Do I deserve this treatment? Have I not sacrificed my young and ardent admirers for your sake? Have I not crushed out the brightness and gayety of my young life to settle down, and become the slave of a man old enough to be my father? For what? To have your confidence withheld from me —

*Mr. G.*   Sue —

*Mrs. G.*   Silence, Mr. Graylock! When I fondly hoped, in making our Alice happy, to brighten our home with the presence of gay, lively company —

*Mr. G.*   Susan —

*Mrs. G.*   Silence, sir! I must be content with your company; not even allowed to share your confidence. You ought to be ashamed of yourself. I wonder your iron-gray locks do not turn white with shame. They look streaked enough. You want to dye them. You'd better. Disguise yourself somehow. Keep out of my sight, for I'm thoroughly ashamed of you. Come, Alice, I'll not waste my time with such a wretch.

*Alice.*   But, Aunt Susy, my marriage —

*Mrs. G.*   Must wait till my lord and master concludes to give his third reason. O Simon, Simon! you've broken my heart. (*Weeps.*) You — you — you've br-br-br-oken my heart.

[*Exit, R., followed by* ALICE.

*Mr. G.* (*looks off* R., *then speaks slowly*). Well,
I never! Bless my soul! Goodness gracious! Heavens
and earth! Here's a tornado, an earthquake, a hurri-
cane! The wife of my bosom, the partner of my joys,
in the enjoyment of a season of calm and tranquil
delight, gets up, and — Well, well, here's blighted
hearthstones, blasted happiness, and for what? For
an untold reason. Make public that reason? disclose
it to the partner of my joys? Never! distinctly, em-
phatically, and unequivocally, never! Tell her that I
oppose my niece's marriage because upon that marriage I, her lawful guardian, must pay into her hands
the sum of ten thousand dollars, left in my hands by
my deceased brother, her father, to be so paid on the
occurrence of her marriage, which marriage must have
my consent? Never! She would drive me from her
presence with scorn, — or any thing else that was handy.
I can't part with the money now. This unlucky,
happy day must be kept far, far away. But my wife,
she must be appeased. How can I bring back her
smiles? Ah, "The Magic Dye!" She would see man-
hood in its prime, raven locks, and all that sort of
thing, about her home. She shall. I will disguise
myself. The die is cast. She will be pleased with
the change: she can't help it. The smile will return
to her rosy lips, and all be bright again. Wilkins can
transform me in five minutes. He shall. I shall dye
happy, and live happy ever after. (*Strikes bell.*) I'll
make a confidant of Bounce. No, I won't. I'll mys-
tify him to — (*Enter* BOUNCE L.)

*Bounce.* Did you ring, sir?

*Mr. G.*   Bounce, I am about to commit a desperate act.

*Bounce.*   Hanother? Why, you've only been married *h*a month!

*Mr. G.*   I am about to leave this home, to go — no matter where; to do — no matter what. You are a faithful servant. You will keep my secret. (*Aside.*) I know he won't.

*Bounce.*   *H*as the *h*apple of my *h*eye, when I know it.

*Mr. G.*   When your mistress asks for me, you will say — nothing; when they search for me, you will lead them to the — well; you will lead them somewhere, anywhere, but where I am — where I go to dye. You understand. Silence, remember. I was here. I am gone, silently, mysteriously (*creeps to door*, R.), like the expiring flame of a candle. Puff! I'm gone.

[*Exit* R.

*Bounce.*   My *h*eyes! master's *h*out of 'is 'ead. 'E's gone off' suiciding, *h*as sure *h*as *h*eggs. 'Ere's *h*a situation for *h*a 'ouse'old. What's to be done? 'E must be stopped, but 'ow? *H*i'll call mistress. Oh, 'ere she *h*is! (*Enter* MRS. GRAYLOCK R.)

*Mrs. G.*   *H*as your master gone out, John?

*Bounce.*   *H*o, mistress, *h*i'm *h*all *h*amstrung. 'E's hout of 'is 'ead, 'e *h*is. 'E's gone somewhere, *h*and 'e's going to do something *h*awful, — put a *h*end to 'imself. *H*it's 'orrible!

*Mrs. G.*   What do you mean?

*Bounce.*   'E said *h*i must lead you to the well. 'E's going to drown 'imself, *h*only the well is dry, *h*and he can't. Perhaps 'e's going to the stable to sacrifice 'imself *hon* the 'alter. *Ho, hit's* 'orrible!

*Mrs. G.* Nonsense, Bounce; he's gone out for a walk.

*Bounce.* Yes, *han' 'e'll* walk *hinto* 'is grave, *han'* then 'e'll walk nights, and scare us to death. *Ho, hit's* 'orrible!

*Mrs. G.* John Bounce, have you been drinking?

*Bounce.* *Hi* 'ave, hi 'ave; tea, green tea; Young 'yson. *Ho,* you'll never set your young *heyes hon's* noble form *hagain.* 'E's gone to die.

*Mrs. G.* Gone to die? I see it all: the wretch!

*Bounce.* So do *hi,* missus, — 'is cold remains, *ha* long procession. Poor master! 'is *hown* 'osses will never carry 'im *hagain!*

*Mrs. G.* John Bounce, you are a fool! Stop your snivelling, and listen to me. Your master has no thought of taking his life. He is bound on a very foolish errand, the purport of which I know. As he has tried to frighten us, we will endeavor to turn the tables upon him. Call Patty.

*Bounce.* Yes, ma'am. You're sure 'e's not gone *hinsane?*

*Mrs. G.* So sure of it that I shall prevent his entrance to the house for the present. You will lock all the doors, and fasten the windows, except one in the kitchen. When you have done that, go to his room, get his rifle, and return here.

*Bounce.* My *heyes!* what *his* coming to this 'ouse? *Ho, hit's* 'orrible! [*Exit* R.

*Mrs. G.* So my good husband, evidently vexed at

my assumed anger, is about to execute his threat of dyeing. Let me see if I cannot turn this to good account, and fix the day for Alice's marriage. That third reason seems to be the impediment; but, if I cannot find that out, I will at least gain his consent by stratagem. O my good Simon! if I cannot win your confidence, I will teach you such a lesson that you will never say dye again. (*Enter* Patty r.)

*Mrs. G.*  Patty.

*Patty.*  Yes, ma'am.

*Mrs. G.*  I believe you are very fond of romantic adventures.

*Patty.*  Indeed, I am, ma'am, though I never had one in my life.

*Mrs. G.*  I am about to throw one in your way. Mr. Graylock will soon return to the house in disguise; that is, he has gone to have his hair and beard dyed. I have given orders to have the doors and windows locked. He will gain an entrance, after some difficulty, to this room. Once here, John Bounce and you, with doors locked, must keep guard over him. Whatever he may say or do, you must not recognize him as your master, but treat him as a burglar. You understand?

*Patty.*  Indeed I do. Trust me to treat him as a burglar. I'll pound him with the broom, and John shall fire a few bullets into him to keep him quiet.

*Mrs. G.*  No, no: there must be no violence. I rely upon your discretion. You are both old servants of his, and will not fail to treat him respectfully. It's only a frolic of his young wife, at which he will laugh heartily when it is over. (*Bell rings.*) There's the bell. Should it be he, do not open the door.

*Patty.* I will remember. [*Exit* R.

*Mrs. G.* Now, then, to rehearse my part in the grand tragedy. (*Enter* PATTY R.)

*Patty.* Mr. Cheeny, ma'am. (*Enter* MR. CHEENY R.)

*Mrs. G.* Ah, Ralph; welcome! [*Exit* PATTY R.

*Ralph* (*shaking hands*). My dear Mrs. Graylock, this is jolly, to see you in such good spirits. Am I right? You have succeeded? (MRS. G. *shakes her head.*) No?

*Mrs. G.* No, my dear friend; the enemy is still strongly intrenched behind the bulwarks of obstinacy, from which neither smiles, tears, nor reproaches can drive him.

*Ralph.* And the assailing party, discomfited, is about to retire from the contest?

*Mrs. G.* Never! We have inscribed upon our banners the motto, "Never say die!"

*Ralph.* Good! You're the best friend a man ever had. But where's Alice? (*Enter* ALICE L.)

*Alice.* O Ralph, it's all over! He'll never give his consent.

*Ralph.* Then, my dear Alice, we will do without it. An unexpected turn in business affairs to-day has made me as independent as a nabob. I should have liked your crusty old uncle's blessing; but, as he won't give it, we'll see Parson Clark, say next Tuesday, be married, take a journey to Niagara, and, on our return, settle quietly into married life. What's to hinder?

*Mrs. G.* The crusty old uncle's wife.

9

*Ralph.* Eh, my dear Mrs. Graylock! A thousand pardons for my levity. He is crusty, you are lovely. "In contrasts lieth love's delight," you know. You will place no bar to our union.

*Mrs. G.* Stop. We have begun a battle: let's fight it out. If Alice marries without her *crusty* old uncle's consent, where's her fortune?

*Ralph.* Her fortune? I never knew she had one. "Her face is her fortune."

*Mrs. G.* With ten thousand dollars with which to buy mirrors to see it in if she please.

*Alice.* Why, Aunt Susy! I never heard of it.

*Mrs. G.* Nor I. But it's true, for I've seen the papers. 'Twas left you by your father, to be paid when you should marry with Mr. Graylock's consent.

*Ralph.* Why, this is charming!

*Alice.* Do you think you like me any better, Ralph?

*Ralph.* Ten thousand times! That is, you understand, I'm not mercenary; but you deserve it, you're such a dear, sweet, nice —

*Mrs. G.* Attention, company! Business! I am going to gain his consent. Ralph, sit at that table, and write, if you please.

*Ralph* (*sits at table;* ALICE *leans on his chair;* MRS. G. *stands* L. *of table*). Yes: proceed.

*Mrs. G.* "I, Simon Graylock, being in sound mind and body" — (*Bell rings.*) Hark! that's he. Don't mind. Write.

*Ralph.* "Sound mind and body."

*Mrs. G.* "Hereby bequeath to my dearly-beloved friend, Ralph Cheeny" — (*Bell rings violently.*)

*Ralph.* " Beloved friend, Ralph Cheeny." Go on.

*Mrs. G.* " My affectionate niece, Alice Chase " — (*Bell rings violently.*)

*Ralph.* " Alice Chase : " that's you, Ally. Go on.

*Mrs. G.* " To have and to hold, as his lawful wife, from this day forth and forevermore. And to this union I give my consent, and subscribe my name." That's all. He has stopped ringing. (*Dog barks.*)

*Mr. G.* (*outside*). Hero, Hero, old boy, don't you know your master? (*Dog barks. Shouting.*)

*Mrs. G.* He's getting into the garden : he will soon be here. We must retire.

*Ralph.* But what is it all about?

*Mrs. G.* Ask no questions. Let me arrange that paper. I will turn the writing underneath, leaving a blank space for his signature. (*Dog barks.*)

*Mr. G.* Clear out, you brute! There goes my coat! Murder! help!

*Ralph.* Shall I run to his assistance?

*Mr. G.* Not for the world! Come this way. I will explain all. [*Exeunt* R. *Then enter, hurriedly,* L., MR. G., *his hair and beard dyed black, one coat-tail, torn off, in his hand.*]

*Mr. G.* Confound that dog! He has decidedly curtailed my enjoyment. (*Holds up coat-tail.*) Is it possible I am so transformed as to become a terror to my own terrier? Where is everybody? Doors locked, windows fastened, and nobody to let me into my own house! A pretty state of affairs, truly! No matter: I have gained an entrance, and now for a good surprise. (*Takes hand-mirror from table.*) What a

change! The Simon Graylock of twenty-five takes
the place of the Simon Graylock of fifty. Glorious!
Won't I make a sensation? I can see my wife's look
of astonishment and pleasure. I can hear her raptur-
ous "O Simon, you beauty!" Eh? what's that?.
(*Turns to* L., *as* JOHN BOUNCE *enters, locks the door,
and stands with his rifle at "present."*) Well, what's
the matter? Eh! what's that? (*Turns* R., *as* PATTY
*enters, locks the door, and stands with a broom at
"present."*) What's the meaning of this?

*Bounce.* Silence! Not *h*a sound! not *h*a step!
Sh — !

*Patty.* Silence! Not a look! not a breath! Sh — !

*Patty and John* (*together*). If you move, if you
speak, you are a dead man. Sh — !

*Mr. G.* Why, John! Patty! you idiots! don't you
know your master?

*Patty and John* (*together*). Master! you! Ha,
ha, ha!

*Mr. G.* Now stop that duet, or out of this house
you go without warning. Unlock those doors, and
call your mistress.

*Bounce.* Call the police. *H*i know you? You're
*h*a burglar, *h*a thief! But we're wide *h*awake. You're
caught.

*Patty.* Yes, Mr. Jack Sheppard, your foot's in the
trap. You've lost your coat-tails, but that's nothing
to the loss of your liberty: ten years in prison.

*Mr. G.* Am I awake? John Bounce, who's your
master?

*Bounce.* Simon Graylock, *H*esquire, *h*a respectable,

middle-*h*aged gent, rather plain *h*in 'is *h*external *h*appearance, but with *h*an 'art *h*as big *h*as an *h*ox.

*Patty.* Yes, Mr. Burglar, as nice an old gentleman as you ever met.

*Mr. G.* Am not I that gentleman?

*Patty.* You! Nonsense!

*Bounce.* You! *H*absurd! Why, you look like what you *h*are, — *h*a regular 'ousebreaker.

*Mr. G.* I'll break your head if you call me that name again. I am master of this house; and as such I order you instantly to unlock those doors, and call your mistress.

*Patty.* What impudence!

*Bounce.* *H*and what *h*assurance!

*Mr. G.* (*approaching Patty*). Young woman, out of my way!

*Patty* (*points broom at him*). Help! murder! thieves!

*Bounce* (*points rifle at him*). 'Ere, you, none er that! Lay *h*a finger *h*on that young woman, *h*and I'll fire. (Mr. G. *backs up stage; they follow with their weapons pointed at him.*)

*Mr. G.* Confound it! this is ridiculous! Go away. (*Gets up into chair.*)

*Bounce.* Wretched *h*outcast, would you lift your 'and *h*against *h*a woman? Would you —

*Mr. G.* Put down that gun.

*Bounce.* Never! You *h*exhasperate the British lion; you *h*insult the *h*object of my 'art's *h*adoration; you — you — you —

*Mr. G.* Put down that gun. It might go off.

9*

*Bounce.* Hit might; but you can't. — Patty, hi'll put *han hend* to 'is miserable *hexistence.*

*Patty.* No; leave him to the officer of justice.

*Bounce.* Hi can't. 'E 'as *kinsulted* you, hand hi must 'ave blood, blood, blood!

*Mr. G.* Put down that gun! Here, Sue! Susan! Susannah! Help! help! help! (*Knock at door,* L.)

*Mrs. G.* (*outside*). Open the door, Patty. (PATTY *unlocks the door,* R. MRS. G., ALICE, *and* RALPH *enter, stand huddled by the door.*) Have you got him?

*Mr. G.* Got him! And she the wife of my bosom! Susy!

*Bounce.* Silence! (*Threatens with gun.*)

*Mr. G.* Susan!

*Patty.* Silence! (*Flourishes broom.*)

*Mr. G.* Susannah!

*Mrs. G.* Why, the wretch knows my name!

*Mr. G.* Of course he does. 'Tis I, your own true, loving husband, Simon Graylock.

*Ralph.* Egad, the rascal has assurance!

*Mrs. G.* Did you ever?

*Alice.* No, I never.

*Mr. G.* (*Coming forward*). Oh, come! this is all nonsense, you know. You're not going to cut me off, are you? I am your husband.

*Mrs. G.* My husband! Why, he's old enough to be your father.

*Mr. G.* (*aside*). There's a " puff" for " The Magic Dye." (*Aloud.*) You don't know me. Am I, then, so changed?

*Mrs. G.* You look like a burglar.

*Ralph.* What a thievish look there is about his mouth!

*Alice.* And such cunning eyes! Oh, do, Aunt Susy, let John call the police, and have him taken away!

*Mr. G.* It's only the effects of the dye, you know. I've had my hair and whiskers colored. Gives me quite a juvenile look; quite the dandy, eh?

*Ralph.* Oh! come, sir, this won't do. You have entered this house in search of plunder. Your attempt has been foiled by the keenness of this lady, who, in the absence of her husband, can well protect his treasures.

*Mrs. G.* John, call the police.

*Mr. G.* John, if you do, I'll discharge you without a character. — Susannah, be reasonable. If you don't know me, you must know these clothes. Are they not your husband's?

*Mrs. G.* My husband's? Gracious heaven! I see it all! My husband has been murdered, cruelly murdered! and you have stolen his clothing. Oh, wretched woman that I am! — John, call the police.

*Mr. G.* And I say, no. Confound it! Do you want to drive me out of my senses?

*Mrs. G.* Oh, take me away! My life's in danger. Oh, somebody take me away!

*Ralph.* Fear not, madam. I will protect you. If your husband has gone, you shall find in me a watchful guardian and a trusty friend. Fear not: the miscreant shall not harm you.

*Mr. G.* Confound his impudence! O Susy! what can I do to make you own me? I think I am your husband; in fact, I'm quite sure of it.

*Mrs. G.* Can you write?

*Mr. G.* Write? I signed a check for two hundred dollars, which you now have in your porte-monnaie.

*Mrs. G.* Can you write your name?

*Mr. G.* To be sure I can.

*Mrs. G.* Then write it. I shall recognize my husband's handwriting, I think ; yes, I'm quite sure of it. Write at once : there are pen, ink, and paper.

*Mr. G.* I'll be hanged if I do any such thing! This is absurd, ridiculous!

*Mrs. G.* John, call the police.

*Bounce.* Hinstantly, missus.

*Mr. G.* Stop! I'll write. (*Goes to table*, c.) If ever I'm caught in such a ridiculous position as this, may I be —

*Mrs. G.* (*goes to table*). Here! write your name there.

*Mr. G.* (*sits, takes up pen, then looks up at* Mrs. G., *who stands immovable*). And that's the wife of my bosom, the partner of my joys! and I've got to write my name before — No! I'll be hanged if I do! (*Throws down pen.*)

*Mrs. G.* John, the police.

*Bounce.* Hinstantly, missus. (John *and* Patty L., Frank *and* Alice R.)

*Mr. G.* No. no : I'll sign! (*Writes.*)

*Mrs. G.* (*takes up paper*). What do I see? 'Tis he, my husband, my Simon! (*Throws her arms about his neck, and repeatedly embraces him in a frantic manner.*)

*Ralph.* What do I hear? 'Tis he, your uncle, my Alice! (*Embraces* Alice.)

*Bounce.* Hit's hall hup. 'Tis 'e 'imself, Patty. (*Embraces* Patty.)

*Patty.* Let me alone, you exasperating Englishman! (*Releases herself.*)

*Mr. G.* Confound it! Susy, don't smother me!

*Mrs. G.* O Simon! something's burning! I smell brimstone!

*Mr. G.* Smell fiddlesticks! It's "The Magic Dye." It makes me sick: I wish I was well rid of it. And now be kind enough to tell me the meaning of this. I've been locked out of my house, my clothes lacerated by my dog, been threatened with death by my servant, with the police by my wife; and am threatened with a brain-fever, if I don't know what all this is for.

*Mrs. G.* For the third reason, Simon.

*Mr. G.* Eh? You're not going to bring up that subject again?

*Mrs. G.* Oh, no! that's all settled.

*Mr. G.* Settled? How?

*Mrs. G.* (*takes paper from table, and reads*). "I, Simon Graylock, being in sound mind and body, hereby bequeath to my dearly beloved friend Ralph Cheeny, my affectionate niece Alice Chase, to have and to hold, as his lawful wife, from this day forth and forevermore; and to this union I give my consent, and subscribe my name." Signed, "Simon Graylock."

*Mr. G.* Why, this is a swindle! Obtaining goods under false pretences! And you, the wife of my bosom, the partner — Do you know what this would cost me, were it known?

*Mrs. G.* Yes; ten thousand dollars: Alice's portion.

*Ralph.* Of which she is in no immediate want; in fact, I think I would prefer to leave it in your hands.

*Mr. G.* My dearly beloved, take her, and be happy. When I die, you will find I have not forgotten you.

*Mrs. G.* As did the partner of your joys, the last time you dyed; eh, Simon?

*Mr. G.* My dear, let's change the subject.

*Mrs. G.* If we could only change the color of your hair as easily! Why, Simon, it's purple!

*Mr. G.* Is it? Then don't look at it, don't speak of it; for, if you're not pleased, I have dyed in vain.

*Mrs. G.* No: for it has helped to make two people happy who were dying for each other, helped your dear wife to triumph in a good cause, and helped us all to a little amusement —

*Mr. G.* At my expense. Sue, Susan, Susannah, let's change the subject. Never say die, and I never will.

JOHN BOUNCE *and* PATTY, R. MR. *and* MRS. G., C. RALPH *and* ALICE, L. *Curtain.*

# THE CHAMPION OF HER SEX.

THE CHAMPION OF HER SEX

# THE CHAMPION OF HER SEX.

## (FOR FEMALE CHARACTERS ONLY.)

---

### CHARACTERS.

Mrs. Duplex, a widow with money and a mission.
Mrs. Deborah Hartshorn, her mother.
Florence Duplex, her daughter.
Caroline Duplex, her step-daughter.
Rhoda Dendron, } her friends.
Pollie Nay, }
Katie O'Neil, the cook.
Maggie Donovan, the chambermaid.

---

COSTUMES MODERN AND APPROPRIATE.

---

Scene.. — *Apartment in* Mrs. Duplex's *house. Lounge,*
L. ; *two chairs*, R. ; *table with writing-materials, and*
*an easy-chair*, C.

*Mrs. Hartshorn (outside,* R). Don't tell me, yeou
imperdent thing ! Clear out, I tell yeou !

*Maggie (outside,* R). Faix ! not for the likes av yez,
at all, at all.

*Mrs. H. (outside,* R.). Yeou won't, hay ? We'll see

10                                            109

about it. (*Enter* MAGGIE, R., *followed by* MRS. H., *brandishing a broom.*)

*Maggie.* Aisy, Mrs. Hartshorn, or it's yersilf will be sent to coort for salt and bathery, sure.

*Mrs. H.* Don't care! If I'm sent to prison for life, I mean to have my orders obeyed.

*Maggie.* Faix, an' it's not yersilf is the lady of the house, at all, at all.

*Mrs. H.* Don't make no difference. Yeou take that broom, and sweep out my room, and be quick about it!

*Maggie.* It's warning I'll give to onct the misthress cooms, Mrs. Hartshorn. Faix! there's a power of work in the house, and a heap of misthresses to order about — bad luck to 'em! Niver mind, I'll swape the room; an', if ye find any thing broke, it's not the fault av Maggie Donovan. (*Aside.*) Only jist I'll — I'll have one good crack at her chiny vases, so I will.

[*Exit* L.

*Mrs. H.* (*sits in chair,* C., *takes out her smelling-bottle, removes stopper, places her finger over it, and applies it to her nose, snuffs it, gives a little start, with something between a sigh and an exclamation, sounding like "Kee," accompanying it. This should be repeated wherever the word appears in the dialogue*). Well! if Hannah Merria's heouse ain't a-going to eternal smash, it's not for want er help. Sich actions I never did see. There's that ere cook! If I stick my head into the kitchen (kee), I'm sure to be saluted with the dishcloth; and, if I go up stairs, there's always a broom laying round loose for me to tumble over (kee). For the land of liberty's sake, what's the use of having a home if you don't take care of it? Neow, here's Hannah Merria, whose husband died a year ago, leaving all his property to her, his second wife, and who ought to be the happiest woman in the world in consequence (kee), — not of his death, but the money, — a-prancin' round in perlitical circuses, ravin' like a lunatic about " speers," and " rights," and " sufferings," and leaving her home to take care of itself. She's the queerest young 'un I ever had (kee). (*Enter* CAROLINE, R.)

*Caroline.* What's the trouble, grandmother?

*Mrs. H.* Oh, it's them hired gals, Ca'line. They've made me crazy with their shiftlessness. I do think Hannah Merria might stay at home, and look arter them.

*Caroline.* My good step-mother has other affairs to occupy her time. You know she is one of the leaders of the Female Reform Club.

*Mrs. H.* Then she'd better bring her club home, and trounce these sassy critters into some kind of reform (kee).

*Caroline.* She thinks she is engaged in a noble work. She is the champion of her sex.

*Mrs. H.* Champion fiddlesticks! There's no sense in such carryings-on. What would my old man, Hezekiah Hartshorn (kee) — bless his dear dead and gone memory — have thought if I'd 'a' gone off in this fashion, a meddlin' with things that women don't know nothin' about? When he took me for better or for wus, sez he to me, " Deborah, there's the old homestid, — a snug house and a likely farm, — all ours. Yeou take kere of the house, and I'll take kere of the farm. Outside I'll be master, inside you shall be mistress; and we won't interfere." That's all the bargain we ever made, and we stuck to it. I took good care to make his home pleasant; but meddlin' with his affairs would have ben as rediculous as it would have ben for him to stick his nose into the churn every time I made butter. No, indeed! Let woman do her own work, and leave man to his'n.

*Caroline.* Ah, grandmother, the world has turned over a great many times since your day. Women have acquired larger ideas of usefulness, and have found in intellectual pursuits release from household drudgery. Triumphs in medical practice, and success in the pulpit, have fired them with ambition to take their place beside the sterner sex in those educational, scientific, and political spheres, for which they feel themselves equally well fitted.

*Mrs. H.* (Kee.) Do hear that young 'un talk; and she don't believe a word of it, nuther.

*Caroline.* But my good step-mother does; and, if she can elevate her sex, she is doing a noble work.

*Mrs. H.* Noble cat's foot! If she wants to elervate her sex, as she calls it, let her stay to home, and look after things. If that Katie don't want elervating with a broomstick, then I'm mistaken (kee). Why don't she give you a eddication, instead of keeping you drudging about the house, when you should be at school with Florence? She's got your father's money, and that's all she keres for (kee).

*Caroline.* I am contented, grandmother. I make no complaint.

*Mrs. H.* 'Cause you're meek as Moses. But I'll give her a piece of my mind, you see ef I don't.

*Caroline.* Don't get angry, grandmother. To-day Florence returns after six months' absence at school. Let her find every thing bright and pleasant.

*Mrs. H.* Lor-a-massy! So she does. Well, I'm glad on it. Ef she don't upset things, then I'm greatly mistaken. (*Bell rings*, R.) She's a dear good girl.

*Caroline.* Indeed she is, and deserves all the care and affection bestowed upon her. (*Enter* KATIE, R., *with a scrubbing-brush in her hand.*)

*Katie.* She's coom, ma'am, she's coom, as rosy and bright as a new copper tay-kettle.

*Caroline.* Who? Florence?

*Katie.* Indade, it's the truth ye's spakin'; her own swate silf, Miss Ca'line.

*Caroline.* Glorious news! I must run to her at once. Come, grandmother. [*Exit*, R.

*Mrs. H.* Bless the child! I must go and fix her somethin' warm.

*Katie.* Somethin' warm, is it? Faix, jist kape out av the kitchen, d'ye mind, or it's yersilf will git somethin' warm.

*Mrs. H.* Wal, I never! The airs that these critters do put on (kee)! [*Exit*, R.

*Katie.* Faix, the onld woman's a sore thrial, that she is. There's little chance to kape my sisther Bridget's children in sugar and tay, wid her middlin'. (*Enter* MAGGIE, L., *with a broom.*)

*Maggie.* An' it's mesilf would likes to know what

10*

ye mane by demaining yersilf in this fashion, Kate O'Nail. It's little yez know of itikate.

*Katie.* Och, be aisy wid yer spakin', Maggie Donovan. Itikate, indade!

*Maggie.* Isn't it me privilege to tend the bell, I'd like to know?

*Katie.* To be sure it is. But 'twas the darling Miss Florence rowled up to the door; and would I be afther lavin' her on the stips, an' you in the attic?

*Maggie.* It's a desateful tongue ye have. Don't I know ye'd be afther liftin' yersilf above yer pots and kittles to my place, to betther yer condition?

*Katie.* Betther my condition, is it? Wid what? Swapin' and dustin', and the likes? Niver, at all, at all. When I betther my condition, 'twill be as the widded bride of Terence McFunnigafferty.

*Maggie.* McFunnigafferty! Bad luck to him! he's only a hod-carrier.

*Katie.* He's dacent and respictable; an' it's my belafe, Maggie Donovan, ye'd be glad av me chance. Haven't I seen ye castin' sly looks that way yersilf?

*Maggie.* Oh, murther! An', an' me own b'y, Teddy Murphy, sailin' the thrackless say —

*Katie.* Wid a swateheart in ivery port.

*Maggie.* Och! it's invious ye are, Kate O'Nail; an' it's out av place ye are above the kitchen shtair. Away wid yez to yer pots and kittles! (*Threatening with broom.*)

*Katie.* An' its out av place ye are onywhere. Be off to yer swapin'! (*Threatens with brush. Enter* FLORENCE *and* CAROLINE, R.)

*Florence.* Fie, fie, girls! You're both out of place, quarrelling. Ah, Maggie! I'm glad to meet you again. (*Shakes hands with Maggie.*)

*Maggie.* Thank you, Miss Florence. An' it's a warm welcome home to yez; an' it's glad I am to see yer own bright face once more.

*Florence.* And it's glad I am to be here, Maggie. Now I want you and Katie to get my trunk up stairs. It's not very heavy, and I wish to open it at once.

> "Take it up tenderly,
> Fashioned so slenderly,
> It's fickle and frail."

*Maggie.* Indade, Miss Florence, I'll do my best with the help of very rough company. [*Exit, R.*

*Katie.* Thar's a fling at me! Arrah, I'll give her one thump on the fut with the thrunk. [*Exit, R.*

*Caroline.* Welcome, welcome, welcome home! A thousand times welcome, Florence! Oh! we have missed you very much. (*They sit on lounge, L.*)

*Florence.* I'm glad of that, Carrie, for you will be so glad to see me now that I can have my own way in every thing; and I'm going to spend my time advantageously. I'm going to induce mother to send you with me when I return to school.

*Caroline.* Oh, that would be grand! But I fear you will not succeed.

*Florence.* But I will. You have as much right to the advantages of Rushly Seminary as I; and I will no longer allow you to submit to the cruel treatment you are receiving. You go with me: that's settled. But where's mother?

*Caroline.* At a committee-meeting.

*Florence.* A committee-meeting at eleven o'clock in the forenoon! What important project can take her from home at this hour?

*Caroline.* She is one of the leaders of the Female Reform Club.

*Florence.* What! my mother! You don't mean to say that she has come out for women's rights!

*Caroline.* She has, most decidedly. She gives all her time to the club. She is a very zealous member.

*Florence.* And who takes care of the house?

*Caroline.* It takes care of itself. The mistress away, it is very hard for me to govern affairs; and grandmother does much harm by her kindly-meant interference in household matters.

*Florence.* It's too bad! Does mother speak at public meetings?

*Caroline.* She spoke for the first time last night. There's a report of her speech in the papers. (*Takes paper from table.*) Here it is.

*Florence* (*reads*). "Mrs. Duplex, widow of the celebrated match-manufacturer, whose decease last winter was chronicled in our paper, arose and spoke warmly of the oppression of the female sex. She vehemently asserted their ability to achieve success in any path trodden by man, and eloquently styled herself the champion of her sex in its endeavors to throw off the yoke of bondage, and victoriously array itself by the side of man in his onward march of progress." What nonsense!

*Caroline.* Nonsense, Florence? Then you are not in sympathy with the woman movement.

*Florence.* Yes. Carrie: I am an earnest advocate for reform. Noble women are doing brave work in *educating* our sex to a realizing sense of their power for good in many of the walks of life heretofore kept sacred to the foot of man. But foolish women, who raise the cry of oppression or slavery, are no better than the political demagogues of the other sex, — loud in speech, but dumb in council.

*Caroline.* And so you think mother has made a mistake?

*Florence.* I certainly do. A woman's duty is to care for her household. From what little I have seen since I came home, I am convinced reform is needed here. ( *Bell rings,* R.) If she would elevate her sex, I'm sure she could have no better task than to fit you — who were left penniless on her hands by a thoughtless father — for the station to which you have a right to aspire. (*Enter* MAGGIE. R.)

*Maggie.* If ye plase, Miss Florence, yez frinds, the Misses Nay and Dendron, are below, axin' for yez.

*Florence.* Show them up. Maggie. (*Exit* MAGGIE, R.) I must find some way to rid mother of her delusion.

*Caroline.* I wish you could, Floy, for it is certainly very disagreeable for us who are left at home. (RHODA *and* POLLIE *appear.* R.)

*Rhoda.* May we come in?

*Florence* (*jumping up*). To be sure you may. Rhoda, you dear, dear girl! (*Kissing her.*) Pollie, I'm glad to see you! (*Kissing* POLLIE.)

*Rhoda.*    Saw you come up, and couldn't wait a minute longer; could we, Pollie?

*Pollie.*    No, indeed.  We just dropped every thing, and ran across.  How d'ye do?

*Rhoda.*    Yes; how are ye?  Tell us, quick!

*Pollie.*    Had a splendid time, hey?

*Rhoda.*    Not engaged, are you?

*Pollie.*    What you got new for dresses?  Why, there's Carrie!  (*Shakes hands, and kisses.*)

*Rhoda.*    Well, I declare, Miss Meekness! you are as still as a mouse.  (*Shakes hands, and kisses.*)

*Caroline.*    She's here, girls, and just as splendid as ever.

*Rhoda and Pollie* (*together*).    Splendid?  Of course she is.

*Florence.*    Come, come, girls; sit down and tell me the news.  (CAROLINE *and* RHODA *sit on lounge*, L.; POLLIE *in chair*, R.; FLORENCE *in chair*, C.)  I'm dying to know what has been going on since I left.

*Pollie.*    Well, then, Tilly Dodd's really married.

*Rhoda.*    Pooh! that's an old story.  She's talking about getting divorced now.

*Pollie.*    Divorced!  Why, she's only been married six months!

*Rhoda.*    Six months and ten days.  No matter about her.  Have you read your mother's speech?

*Florence.*    I read a brief notice of it.

*Rhoda.*    I heard it all.  She's the champion of her sex.  Oh, it was grand!  She flourished her right hand as majestically as any orator I ever heard; and her voice was as strong and clear as Patrick Henry's.

*Pollie.* Lor, Rhoda, you never heard Patrick Henry.

*Rhoda.* But I've read his speeches, and they've got the ring of his voice in them yet. Ain't you proud of your mother, Flory?

*Florence.* Not of her last effort, Rhoda.

*Pollie.* That's where you're right, Floy. I wouldn't like to have my mother spouting in that manner. It looks coarse and unladylike.

*Rhoda.* Well, I don't think I should like to have my mother take to that kind of business.

*Florence.* I like it so little, girls, that I am determined to give mother a lesson, if you will grant me your assistance. Our principal, Miss Steady, had an attack of "woman's rights" at school last winter; and the girls took advantage of it to indulge in a little masquerading, which so affected our honored head, that we heard no more of woman's rights for the balance of the term. I shouldn't wonder if something of the kind would make mother a little less zealous in the cause.

*Rhoda.* Oh, tell us all about it!

*Pollie.* Is there any fun in it?

*Florence.* You shall see. Come to my room. Mother may return at any moment, and I do not wish her to see us at present.

*Pollie.* There's something delightfully mysterious in your proceedings, Floy.

*Rhoda.* Yes: there's mischief in your eyes.

*Florence.* Perhaps; time will show. Come, I want you too, Carrie. [*Exeunt*, R., FLORENCE, RHODA, *and* POLLIE.]

*Caroline.* Take me with her! I wish she could. I

love Floy too well to envy her. But the privileges she enjoys, and to which I feel I am entitled, would afford me those opportunities for culture for which I have often sighed. (*Enter* Mrs. Duplex.)

*Mrs. D.* Caroline, I am astonished! You sitting here with your arms folded, and the house in disorder! Is this a fitting return for my care? or have you forgotten that to me you owe all you have in the world?

*Caroline.* You never allow me to forget that, madam. Yet I am grateful for your care. Add one favor more, and let me go into the world, and earn my living.

*Mrs. D.* Indeed! As you are anxious to earn a living, perhaps it would be as well to commence at home.

*Caroline.* This life is distasteful —

*Mrs. D.* There, that's quite enough. I have very important business to engage my attention. Set the reception-room in order at once. (*Takes off bonnet and shawl, and sits in easy-chair near table.*)

*Caroline.* Certainly, madam.    [*Exit,* R.

*Mrs. D.* My late lamented husband left me one useless incumbrance, — that girl. Strange some people are so hard to manage! Now, then, to business. I've a long report to make to-night on the "Scheme for Improving the Condition of Motherless Girls." (*Enter* Mrs. Hartshorn, R.)

*Mrs. H.* Lor, sakes, Hannah Merria! You home?

*Mrs. D.* Yes, mother, and hard at work.

*Mrs. H.* (*sitting on lounge, and knitting*). Du tell!

*Mrs. D.* Yes, mother. There's a wide field of

labor opening to willing hands. To raise woman from her lowly position, is not that most noble work?

*Mrs. H.* That depends on what she's doing, Hannah Merria. If she's scrubbing the floor (kee), the lower the better.

*Mrs. D.* She was never meant for such ignoble toil.

*Mrs. H.* Ignoble fiddlesticks! P'r'aps you want the men-folks to do that.

*Mrs. D.* It may be necessary for the triumph of woman. Did you read my speech, mother?

*Mrs. H.* No, I didn't. I've *heard* enough on 'em to be heartily sick. A pretty champion of your sex, you are!

*Mrs. D.* I hope I am an earnest and an honest one. I have a mission, — to lift woman to a higher plane of civilization; and I believe I have the power to fulfil it.

*Mrs. H.* How? By getting up and speaking out in meeting? Never heard nothin' like it since Sally Skreecher j'ined the Millerites, and hollered so in meetin', that they thought the Angel Gabriel was a-tootin' his horn (kee.)

*Mrs. D.* Ah, mother! you do not understand this noble movement of woman.

*Mrs. H.* I understand washin' and ironin', and that's what I call the noblest movement woman ever took a hand in.

*Mrs. D.* There; that's quite enough: we shall never agree. Be quiet, and let me write.

*Mrs. H.* (Kee.)

11

*Mrs. D.* (*writes*). " Silently, but steadily, moves on the mighty car of progress " —

*Mrs. H.* (Kee.)

*Mrs. D.* " Crushing, beneath its fast revolving wheels, prejudice and wrong; upward soars the spirit of freedom, mounting on eagles' wings."

*Mrs. H.* (Kee.) Say goose's wings, Hannah Merria.

*Mrs. D.* Mother, will you be silent?

*Mrs. H.* And hear you talk that bosh? Why, every Fourth-of-July speaker has said them things year after year since Cornwallis surrendered. (*Enter* RHODA, R., *disguised; a black shawl pinned tightly across her breast; faded black bonnet with bright flowers stuck in it; large, black cotton gloves, much too long in the fingers, on her hands; and parasol.*)

*Rhoda* (*very extravagant in her gestures*). Where is she? Let me look upon her, the deliverer of our race, the champion of our sex! Ah, she's here! the noble face, the stately figger! 'Tis she! 'tis she! (*Falls at the feet of* Mrs. D.)

*Mrs. H.* Land er Goshen! that's Hannah Dudley!

*Mrs. D.* My good woman, can I be of service to you?

*Rhoda* (*rises*). You can, you can. I am the mother of nine interesting children, whom I have vainly endeavored to support for five years by the manufacture of molasses-candy. A sweet occupation, but, alas! not profitable; for, work as I will, I can make but just enough to satisfy the wants of my children. 'Tis all they have for food.

*Mrs. H.* Well, they're a sweet set.

*Mrs. D.*   My good woman, why do you come to me?

*Rhoda.*   I come to sit at your feet; to draw into my thirsty soul the teachings of your stupendous intellect. Glorious champion of my sex, I would wrest from proud man one of his boasted prerogatives.

*Mrs. D.*   Indeed! To what sphere of usefulness do you aspire?

*Mrs. H.*   She's ravin' about paregoric. She ought to be a doctor.

*Rhoda.*   I heard your glorious speech last night, and every fibre of my being thrilled beneath the touch of your matchless eloquence. You told us we had the ability to achieve success in any occupation where man could triumph. I want to be a butcher.

*Mrs. H.*   Heavens and airth! the woman's loony!

*Rhoda.*   Yes, a butcher; that I may give my children strong food, for which they hanker. Ah, the mighty butcher! the crafty butcher! the skilful butcher! I have gazed upon him with admiration. With what power he fells the mighty oxen and — and — things! How skilfully he sends to "green fields and pastures new" the sportive lambs! With what grace he seizes the portly hog, and, regardless of its piteous cries, ends its devouring life! Oh, glorious champion of our sex, teach me to excel in this great branch of usefulness, and fill the mouths of my babes!   ·

*Mrs. D.*   Woman, have you escaped from a lunatic asylum?

*Mrs. H.*   Lor, Hannah Merria, she's 'sterricky.

*Mrs. D.*   The poor woman's mad.

*Rhoda.*   Mad? Then 'tis you who have made me

so. You promise, and do not fulfil. Make me a
butcher, or I will proclaim you a traitor to our cause,
from the market-place, in the council-hall, from the
house-tops. Champion of the sex! Bah! Give my
children beef, pork, mutton, or "get you to a nun-
nery," quick.                                    [*Exit*, R.

*Mrs. D.*  Poor woman, poor woman!

*Mrs. H.*  Nothin' but skin and bones (kee). This
all comes of political circuses. O Hannah Merria!
the millinariam won't come any sooner for all yer
speechifyin'. Better stay to home. Lor sakes! who's
this? (*Enter* POLLIE, *disguised. Old-fashioned straw
bonnet, bright ribbons; faded shawl of bright patterns;
white cotton gloves, very large, upon hands.*)

*Pollie.*  W-w-where is she, — the ch-ch-champion
of our s-s-s-s-sex?

*Mrs. D.*  What do you wish, good woman?

*Pollie.*  'T-t-tis she: I know th-th-th-that v-v-voice!
D-d-dear Mrs. D-D-Duplex, last night you m-m-moved
me with the f-f-f-force of your el-l-l-oquence. I have
long b-b-blushed at our de-p-p-p-pendent situation: I
have thrown off the c-ch-chain, and stand p-p-prepared
to wrest from man one of his pr-p-proud p-p-p-p-pre-
rogatives.

*Mrs. H.*  There's an awful waste of paregoric there.

*Mrs. D.*  And pray, my good woman, to what new
field of labor do you aspire?

*Pollie.*  B-b-before I heard your v-voice, I listened
to one that charmed my f-f-f-fancy. M-m-make me
like him, and I will b-b-bless you. I would be an auc-
sh-sh-shuneer.

*Mrs. D.* An auctioneer! do you want to insult me?

*Pollie.* Insult you, the ch-ch-champion of our s-s-s-sex? N-n-never! B-b-but an auc-sh-sh-shuneer I must be. G-g-going, g-g-going, g-g-gone. Oh, it's splendid! How much am I offered? St-st-stove, t-t-table, ch-chair, in one l-l-lot. H-h-how much? G-g-going, g-going —

*Mrs. H.* (Kee.)

*Pollie.* G-g-gone! Thank you, marm.

*Mrs. D.* Woman, leave this house at once!

*Pollie.* What f-f-for? Ain't you the ch-ch-champion of our s-s-sex? D-d-didn't you s-s-say we were f-f-f-fitted to t-t-take the place of m-m-man? and ain't I g-g-going to be an auc-sh-shuneer, hey?

*Mrs. D.* You are fit for nothing but the workhouse. Instantly leave this room, or I will have you driven into the street.

*Pollie.* Ch-ch-champion of our s-s-sex! P-p-pooh! You're an imp-p-postor: you d-d-deceive us with your sp-p-peeches. If you don't make me an auc-sh-sh-shuneer, I'll d-denounce you, — yes, I will, now, at once. I'm g-g-going, g-g-going, g-gone.   [*Exit*, R.

*Mrs. D.* Was there ever any thing so provoking? It's the work of our enemies.

*Mrs. H.* No, 'tain't, Hannah: it's a nat'ral impediment.

*Mrs. D.* Mother, shut up!

*Mrs. H.* Wal, I never! Is that the way you honor your parent? (Kee.)

*Mrs. D.* It seems I am to be made a laughing-

stock for my speech.  Could I have been too hasty?
(*Enter* FLORENCE, R.)

*Mrs. D.* Goodness, child! you home again? (*Rises.*)

*Florence* (*tragically*).   Stop!  Approach me not.
Busy rumor, with its thousand tongues, says, last
night you asserted, in a crowded assembly, that
woman could achieve success in any path trodden by
man.  I come to you for truth.  Speak, mother! did
you speak those words? is rumor true?

*Mrs. D.* I did say so, Florence.

*Florence* (*lightly*).  Then, my good mother, you
will be delighted to hear that your daughter has chosen
the profession in which she hopes to win fame.  I want
to be a lawyer.

*Mrs. H.* Lor sakes!

*Mrs. D.* Florence, you are trifling with a serious
matter.

*Florence.* Yes, 'tis a serious matter.  But I feel
that in that profession I can win success.  "Gentlemen of the jury, I stand before you to plead the cause
of a young girl, who needs all your sympathy.  She
was the idol of fond parents: but, alas! her mother
died: her father took to his side a second bride, and
she was neglected.  Not content with this, on his
death-bed the father cut her off from any share of his
wealth, and left to the mercy of her step-mother."

*Mrs. D.* Florence, what means this?

*Florence.* "Gentlemen of the jury, can you ask?
Beneath this roof is one who is entitled to all the
benefits of wealth and education; but she is made a
drudge: while she who should rear her tenderly sees

not the oppressed in her own home, but seeks abroad that labor for the improvement of the condition of motherless girls which should be commenced beneath her own roof."

*Mrs. D.*   Florence, are you serious, or are you crazy?

*Mrs. H.*   Not a bit of it, Hannah Merria (*kee*).

*Florence.*   Only   practising,   mother.   (*Enter* RHODA, R.)

*Rhoda.*   Mrs. Duplex, champion of our sex, I want to be an actor!

*Mrs. D.*   An actress, you mean.

*Rhoda.*   No, an actor.   Richard the Third, Richelieu, Macbeth, are the characters I would play.   They are manly.   If man can excel in them, so can woman. Have you not said we could win success —

*Mrs. D.*   Silence!   Don't let me hear that word again.

*Rhoda.*   Yes: let me tread the boards as Macbeth.

"Is this a dagger which I see before me?"

*Mrs. H.*   (Kee.)   That young one's loony too.

*Rhoda.*   Or as Richelieu.

"In the lexicon of youth, which Fate preserves for a bright
      manhood,
   There's no such word as fail!"

*Mrs. H.*   (Kee.)   Mad as a March hare!

*Rhoda.*   Or as Richard.

"Off with his head!   So much for Buckingham."

*Mrs. H.*   Land sakes! that would be too much for him.

*Mrs. D.* Enough of this, Rhoda Dendron. I do not care to be made the butt of your amusement. We can dispense with your company. (*Enter* POLLIE, R.)

*Pollie.* Mrs. Duplex, champion of your sex, I have chosen my profession. I will be a general in the army. .

*Mrs. D.* Pollie Nay!

*Pollie.* A glorious life, at the head of a host, charging upon the foe. "Up and at them!"

"Charge, Chester, charge! On, Stanley, on!"

*Mrs. D.* Silence! Florence, what does all this mean? Gracious goodness! whom have we here? (*Enter* MAGGIE, L., *with a rough pea-jacket and a tarpaulin hat added to her costume.*)

*Mrs. D.* Maggie, what does this mean?

*Maggie.* If ye plaze, missus, they towld me nixt door that all the women-folks was a-goin' to step into the men's places; and so I thought I'd jist give warnin', and take mesilf to the say, for me own Teddy is a sailor, and I might climb the sails, and pull the ropes, and haul in a jib, till I larnt the way, if ye plaze.

*Mrs. D.* Why, Maggie, I'm astounded to think you should listen to such nonsense.

*Maggie.* Sure, 'twas Bridget Daly, nixt door, that heard yez own silf talk last night, and towld me. (*Enter* KATIE, R., *with a large military hat on her head, a gun on her shoulder.*)

*Maggie.* Oh, murther! Here's Kate wid a gun!

*All.* A gun! (KATIE *comes*, C.)

*Pollie* (R.). Oh, dear! put it the other way! (KATIE *turns to* R.)

*Rhoda.* (L.) No, no! the other way!

*Mrs. H.* Lord-a-mercy! she'll blow all our brains out! (*Gets behind lounge.*)

*Florence.* Put down that gun, Katie. (KATIE *takes it from her shoulder.*)

(POLLIE *and* RHODA *scream, and jump up in chairs,* R.; MRS. DUPLEX *gets behind easy-chair;* MAGGIE *jumps upon lounge; and all cry.* "*Drop it!*" "*It's loaded!*" "*Take it away!*" "*Call somebody!*")

*Florence (takes the gun, and lays it upon the floor).* You can descend in safety, girls. (*All get down.*)

*Mrs. D.* Now, Katie, what does this mean?

*Katie.* If ye plaze, Mrs. Duplex, I thought, bein' the good time that's comin' was come, and the women-folks was a goin' to rule, and the men-folks do the housework, I'd give warnin', if you plaze. (*Stoops, and picks up the gun. All scream, and renew their old positions on chairs, behind chair and lounge, as before; repeat cries,* "*Put it down,*" *&c.*)

*Florence.* Don't be alarmed: it's not loaded. (*All quiet again.*)

*Mrs. D.* Well, it's about time an end was put to this nonsense. You have picked up one of my remarks last night for the purpose of laughing at me, or —

*Florence.* Teaching a lesson, mother.

*Mrs. D.* Well, I acknowledge my remarks were a little wild, and am prepared to pay the penance. What shall it be? You seem to have been the manager of the remarkable scene. Speak.

*Florence.* Mother, I want to take Carrie back with me when I return to school.

*Mrs. H.* Bless my soul! what do you think I found in your father's desk to-day? Something that looks, for all the world, like a will. Here it is. (*Gives paper to* Mrs. D.)

*Mrs. D.* A will! (*Opening it.*) And of a later date than the one in my possession. (*Reads.*) "To be equally divided between my dear wife, and my beloved daughter Caroline." Indeed! This must be seen to.

*Florence.* Ah! then Carrie is not penniless, after all.

*Mrs. D.* Florence, how can you speak so? Never, while I live. Where is the dear child?

*Mrs. H.* Shouldn't wonder if she was sweepin' off the steps. (*Enter* CAROLINE, R.)

*Caroline.* The reception-room is in order, madam.

*Mrs. D.* Caroline, my dear child, I think your experience in house-affairs has been sufficient for the present. You will go with my daughter to Rushly Seminary on her return. I shall look after my house myself hereafter.

*Mrs. H.* Lor' sakes, Hannah Merria, are you coming to your senses?

*Mrs. D.* I hope I have never been bereft of them.

*Florence.* And the Reform Club, mother —

*Mrs. D.* Shall still have my hearty support; but no more public speeches for the present, for my house needs putting in order; and you have reminded me of that which I had almost forgotten, that a woman's first duty is to her home.

*Katie.* Faith, ma'am, if there's to be a misthress, I'll sthay, if yez plaze.

*Maggie.* An' mesilf, too, missus, by your lave.

*Florence.* There, mother, the storm's over; so let's hear no more of "woman's rights."

*Rhoda.* And I can't be a butcher!

*Pollie.* Nor I an auc-sh-sh-shuneer. It's too bad!

*Mrs. D.* So there has been masquerading here.

*Florence.* For which I alone am to blame. Mother, we are wild girls, and good subjects for missionary work. Set the Female Reform Club a good example by commencing its work in your own neighborhood, and reform us.

*Mrs. D.* There is certainly a large field of labor here for me; and I shall set about the work at once. But what will the officers of the club say?

*Mrs. H.* (Kee.) That you've backslid, Hannah Merria.

*Florence.* If they are honest and earnest, they will say that she who to the welfare of her family first gives her heart, is a stanch friend to progress. In that realm she is queen, and they who bend beneath her loving sway, freely acknowledge her, in that grand sphere, the Champion of her Sex.

*Situations.*

|  |  |
|---|---|
| CAROLINE. | FLORENCE. |
| RHODA. | MRS. D. |
| POLLIE. | MRS. H. |
| KATIE. | MAGGIE. |
| R. | L. |

*Curtain.*

# THE VISIONS OF FREEDOM.

# THE VISIONS OF FREEDOM.

## A NATIONAL ALLEGORY.

---

### CHARACTERS.

GLORIA, Goddess of Freedom.
RUBINA, her Counsellor of War.
SERENA, her Counsellor of Peace.
QUEEN MAB of Dreamland.
DROWSA, OBLIVIA, SOMNA, SOOTHA, Dream-Spirits.
ART, INDUSTRY, MUSIC, PLENTY, SERENA's Attendants.
REVENGE, DISCORD, CRUELTY, HATRED, RUBINA's Attendants.

---

*Action supposed to have occurred in Dreamland.
Green bank, c. Behind this a small platform about
six inches high; chorus seated R. and L. of stage.*

*Opening Chorus; air, " The Quiet Night."*

Slumber o'er earth is sending
  Its realm of sweet repose :
The stream of life, rest-tending,
  In peace through Dreamland flows ;
Where waiting and caressing,
With varied visions blessing,
  Dream spirits vigils keep ;
  Dream spirits vigils keep ;
  Their vigils keep, their vigils keep.

135

*(As the chorus closes, enter* R., DROWSA *and* OBLIVIA ;
L., SOMNA *and* SOOTHA ; *then* R., QUEEN MAB, *who
stands* C.)


*Q. Mab.*    Spirits of Dreamland, once again we meet,
Our round of nightly revel to repeat.
O'er earth, when locked in sleep's warm, close em-
        brace,
Since time began, the genius of our race
Has had the power fearlessly to sway
The visionary sceptre all obey.
The mighty monarch, who, with tyrant frown,
Upholds the burden of his weighty crown ;
The fierce-browed warrior who relentless slays,
And, bathed in blood, his vows to Moloch pays ;
Haughty and lowly, powerful and weak, —
Under mysterious spells our guidance seek.
Sweet sister spirits, Dreamland opens wide ;
Yet justice guards it well on every side.
Over the pure we rosy visions throw :
Around the base a sea of troubles flow.
Ere forth you glide to ply your happy arts,
Your queen would learn the secrets of your hearts ;
Who hie to sport, with mischievous intent,
And who on graver ministries are bent.
    *Sootha.*    I've an old miser under watchful care,
With sordid soul, of generous impulse bare ;
Who nightly feasts, with avaricious eyes,
Where treasured gold in rare profusion lies ;
Who revels o'er his fast-increasing store,
Chuckles with glee, yet wistful sighs for more ;

Starvation's image, in a den so bare,
It seems a fit abode for dark despair.
Into his sleep I glide, disturb his rest,
Rattle his treasure, till, with fear possessed,
As frightful visions thick and thicker press,
He trembling wakes, his idol to caress.

   *Oblivia.*  Fair queen, a toiling student I enchain,
And with my art refresh his weary brain :
Up wisdom's heights I lead him by the hand,
And show him visions of the promised land ;
Fair fields of learning spread before his gaze,
For him the realm of science set ablaze,
Ope Fame's grand temple, Honor's scroll unroll,
And tell the triumphs of the trusting soul,
Till hope re-animates the wasting fire
With earnest zeal and conquering desire.

   *Somna.*  I guard a trusting maiden, young and
      fair,
Whom Love has tangled in his silken snare ;
Spread rosy dreams amid her sleeping hours,
And lead her captive through a land of flowers ;
Adorn her hero with true manly pride,
And of the future ope the portal wide,
While smiles of pleasure o'er her sweet face creep,
And blissful words betray her secret deep.
With rare delight her day-dreams I repeat,
And make her young life's round of love complete.

   *Drowsa.*  Oh, I've a task, fair queen, will love secure.
Last night I visited with visions pure
A weary mother, who, for many a day,
Watched o'er the cradle where her dear babe lay

12*

Wasting with fever, till the unseen Hand
Took it in kindness to a better land.
Long has she mourned its loss, with wakeful eyes,
Fast-falling tears, low, sad, and bitter cries.
Last night she slept ; and then, in vision's charms,
I crept, and laid her babe within her arms.
Content she rested, with a smile so sweet,
I go to-night this comfort to repeat.

   *Q. Mab.*  Your zeal, industrious spirits, we applaud :
Your chosen missions meet with full accord ;
Yet for this night we have a task so grand,
Your queen would all your energies command.

    *Somna.*   We wait your pleasure,
    *Oblicia.*                              All our arts employ ;
    *Drowsa.*   Set us what tasks you will,
    *Sootha.*                              We'll serve with joy.
    *Q. Mab.*   Thanks, sisters !  To our confidence draw
      near,
And list our secret with attentive ear.
Freedom's fair goddess, Gloria, in doubt,
Her fair Republic, restless roams about,
Seeking a talisman to life prolong,
And make her youthful charge wax brave and strong.
Close at her side Rubina, crafty maid,
Whose fire-lit eyes gloat over war's dread trade,
Plies her bold speech, unchecked by fear of frown,
Counselling deeds of conquest and renown ;
While calm Serena, long to Peace allied,
Whose gentle influence stretches far and wide,
Recounts the glories of a land at rest,
With sterling Industry's rich harvests blest.

Wavering betwixt the gentle and the bold,
By turns rebellious, and by turns controlled,
Poor Gloria wanders long, in dire distress
Which counsellor to choose her realm to bless.
Old custom gives to us prophetic power
To guide by vision in the trying hour.
And so to-night, o'er Gloria's doubting heart,
Fair sister spirits, we will ply our art,
Lure her to Dreamland, and in phantom light
Illume her path, and guide her to the right.
Stand close! she comes! the light winds bear along
The martial burden of her triumph song.

*[Retire, and form behind bank.*

*Chorus; air, " Love of Country."*

Blest is the land where Freedom rears,
   'Neath heaven's blue, arching dome,
For labor's sons of every clime,
   Her proud and happy home.
Beyond the reach of tyrant rule,
   Free are the hands we raise:
Onward we move, with joyous song
   Of thankfulness and praise.
Blest is the land, &c.

*(Enter* L., GLORIA, *attended by* RUBINA *and* SERENA,
*followed by* ATTENDANTS.)

c. GLORIA.

R. RUBINA. SERENA, L.

ATTENDANTS. ATTENDANTS.

*Gloria.* Yes, mine, all mine, this bounteous land,
So rich in varied blessings that command
Homage from all. The mighty of the earth
Must stoop to thee. O land of lowly birth!
Thy mountains rise in majesty and pride;
In royal state thy valleys open wide;
Thy broad, expansive waters, spreading free,
Embrace the bosom of the mother sea;
Out of a fruitful earth thy harvests rise;
Out leaps the golden ore with glad surprise;
Over thy broad domains, with ceaseless hum,
Labor's grand armies ever conquering come;
While rare Invention opes its secret heart,
And Genius rears its monumental art.
O land of promise! Gloria's inmost prayer
Could ask no more than thy fair fate to share.
Sweet counsellors, let Wisdom quick contrive
Some plan this happy state to keep alive.
*Rubina.* A nation's life, fair mistress, action craves;
Cold, sluggish apathy the blood enslaves.

Renown's the rock on which to rear a state;
Rubina's counsel is for conquest straight.

   *Gloria.* Conquest, Rubina! Thine's a sorry jest.
We have no quarrels: friends with all we rest.

   *Rubina.* Ay: but to win renown, with fair excuse,
Strike at the shadow of some old abuse
Among our neighbors; or, with slight parade
Of justice, boldly on their borders raid.
Quick to revenge, their warlike hearts upspring:
"To arms! to arms!" they cry. Their weapons
     ring;
On us they march, a fast-increasing band,
Till in the confines of our realm they stand.
"Quick! to repel invasion!" then our cry:
Alarming signals flash out fierce and high;
From east and west, from north and south, outpour
The sons of Freedom, in their strength secure;
Drive back the foe, in turn invade their fold,
Until their fate victoriously we hold.

   *Gloria.* And then—

   *Rubina.* And then boldly for ransom claim
A portion of their realm in Freedom's name.

   *Gloria.* What says Serena?

   *Serena.* 'Tis a crafty plot,
And full of wickedness. I like it not.
Freedom's a name too sacred to infold
A hungering appetite for greed and gold.
What conquest gains is ne'er enriched by toil;
Ensanguined earth is but a sterile soil.
Rubina's counsel, and her bold device,
Would purchase glory at a bloody price.

*Rubina.*   Serena, pause! thou hast no right to frown,
With thy cold-hearted words, my counsel down.
No crafty plot I weave to bring disgrace,
But lofty plans to glorify the race.
Let War once set his standard in the field,
With strength and valor blazoned on his shield,
The roar of cannon, and the clash of steel,
Shall glad the nation with triumphant peal,
And strong and mighty conquerers enroll
Heroic deeds on her historic scroll.

    *Serena.*   While o'er the land the blood of her dear
        sons —
Conquest's sad recompense — in horror runs.
Forbear, Rubina!   Gracious mistress, might
Should ever wield its strong arm for the right.
Let not Rubina's counsel carry weight,
Lest angry discord rend your lofty state.

    *Rubina.*   Insult again —

    *Gloria.*              Nay, nay, Rubina.   Pause:
Thou hast had ample time to urge thy cause.
With patience curb a while thy fiery mood;
We'll ponder well thy influence for good.
Speak thou, Serena.   Canst thou find release
For our perplexity in ways of peace?

    *Serena.*   Ay, peace, fair mistress, is the fount of
        health,
Whence flow the streams of happiness and wealth
That bless a nation.   In its waters fair,
Drowned are the pangs of life-corroding care;
Cheered and refreshed is duty's faithful heart,
In labor's trials strong to take its part.

O happy Gloria! o'er this blest domain,
With Peace thy minister, forever reign.
Its power can bless thy state with bright renown,
And deck with radiant gems thy royal crown.
Let not bold War thy quiet glades invade,
To ruthless revel in thy marts of trade,
Affront thy people with its thundering peal,
And grind the harvests 'neath its iron heel.
For Peace is mighty to achieve all ends,
And highest good with grandest triumph blends.

 *Rubina.* Ignoble Toil, Serena, grovels low,
And on the race no glory can bestow.

 *Serena.* Toil is the power that tears the rock away,
And brings rare jewels to the light of day.

 *Rubina.* 'Tis base!

 *Serena.*     'Tis noble!

 *Gloria.*       Silence, I entreat!

Counsel is vain when angry passions meet.
In patience we have heard: in patience wait,
Till we have pondered on this strange debate,
And made our choice. Anon we'll make it known.
Await our pleasure. We would be alone.


(*Repeat chorus, "Blest is the land," &c., and march
 off* R., RUBINA *and* ATTENDANTS; L., SERENA *and*
 ATTENDANTS. GLORIA *sits on bank.*)


 *Gloria.* O doubting heart! the battle to repeat,
Within thy depths Content and Conquest meet.
Upon the field where Conscience sits enthroned,
One must be victor crowned, and one disowned.

When Wisdom all its arguments hath plied,
Thou, judge impartial, must the case decide.
Upon thy fiat hangs a nation's fate:
Give me the power to make my people great.

*Song; air, " Oh, come ye into the summer woods:"*
    QUEEN MAB *and* DREAM-SPIRITS.

> Oh, sink you into soft slumber's arms!
>     There dwelleth no annoy;
> There freely rove the Dreamland sprites,
>     And sweet rest is full of joy.
> *Gloria (slowly sinks to rest, speaking softly, with
>     closed eyes).*
Soft, drowsy spirits o'er my senses creep,
And bear me captive to the realm of sleep.

*Song continued.*

> We'll spread for you, in phantom light,
>     That plainly you may know,
> The woes of dreadful warfare,
>     The joys from peace that flow.
> Oh! sink you, &c.

Queen *Mab (comes front of bank, and kneels;*
SOMNA *and* OBLIVIA *come down* R.; DROWSA *and*
SOOTHA, L.).

Ay, sink to sleep, fair goddess. Healthy rest
From weighty care shall ease thy troubled breast;
Prophetic visions o'er thy senses roll,
To guide to just result thy struggling soul.

Rubina comes with treason in her tread,
To crafty acts by false ambition led.


(*Enter* RUBINA, R. *She passes behind bank, and stands
c., looking down at* GLORIA. *Then enter* R., CRUELTY
*and* HATRED, *who pass to* L. ; DISCORD *and* REVENGE,
*who stand* R.)

RUBINA.
GLORIA, *on bank.*
QUEEN MAB, *kneeling.*

| R. DISCORD. | HATRED. L. |
|---|---|
| SOMNA. | SOOTHA. |
| REVENGE. | CRUELTY. |
| OBLIVIA. | DROWSA. |


*Rubina.* In fetters bound all powerless she lies,
The mighty goddess who all earth defies,
The slave of sleep. Relinquished the command
Which sways the fortune of her chosen land.
The gleaming crown on her majestic brow
But serves as symbol of her bondage now.
Should I but snatch it from her pillowed head,
Rubina rules, and Freedom's host is led
Instant to conquest. 'Tis a glorious aim.
Speak, you who wait : have I your free acclaim?
    *Discord.* Quick! snatch the crown, and I will hie
      away
To boldly with the meaner passions play ;
Quicken your hosts with feverish desire,
With love of anarchy their bosoms fire.

13

Pause not, but on the instant power assume!
Discord will go before, and cry, " Make room!"
   *Cruelty.*  Ay, wear the crown. Let war defiant
    move;
Let me 'mid soft and tender passions rove,
Crushing and slaying, turning all to steel,
Forged in the flame of fierce and bitter zeal.
Allegiance to thee, Cruelty will give;
Under thy triumphs will she grandly live.
   *Hatred.*  Usurp the regal state, and I am free
War's stanch and sturdy champion to be.
Warm blood I quicken with a thirsty hate,
That nought but anarchy can satiate.
Unto thy crown I full allegiance lend;
Hatred by thee will ever stand as friend.
   *Revenge.*  Success to treason! At thy feet I lay
My fond allegiance. Bid me quick array
The fiercest passions. I will straightway prove
My bold endeavor worthy of thy love.
War is my idol; at its luring call
Revenge is quick, and sure to conquer all
   *Rubina.*  O glorious spirits! what you free ac-
    cord,
This grateful heart shall bless with rich reward.
Success is certain: I'll no longer pause,
But raise aloft the standard of our cause.

     (*Takes crown from* GLORIA's *head.*)

The crown is mine. Rise, War, in triumph now;
Gloria's rare diadem is on my brow!

TABLEAU.    *The crowning of War.*

HATRED.                RUBINA.                DISCORD.
                 GLORIA, *on bank.*

R. SOMNA.              QUEEN MAB.              SOOTHA. L.
  REVENGE.                                    CRUELTY.
  OBLIVIA.                                    DROWSA.

*A chord.* RUBINA *places crown on her head; stands with her hands raised to the crown.* GLORIA *starts up, resting on one hand, her other hand raised to her brow, terror in her eyes.* QUEEN MAB *on her knees in front of bank, her hands clasped, resting in her lap, head thrown back.* SOMNA, R., *and* SOOTHA, L., *in line with* QUEEN MAB, *crouch each with one hand on her shoulder, the other outstretched, as though warding off danger.* HATRED *and* DISCORD *run R. and L. of* RUBINA; *each has hand on her waist, the other raised in triumph.* DROWSA *falls at the feet of* CRUELTY, L., *her back to audience, her hands raised and clasped.* CRUELTY *looks down at her with right hand raised and clenched, as though about to strike.* OBLIVIA *falls at the feet of* REVENGE, R., *with outstretched arms, facing audience;* REVENGE *seizes her hands, bends her back, and looks into her face.* Expressions of terror on the faces of DREAM-SPIRITS *and* GLORIA; *triumph in those of* RUBINA *and her* ATTENDANTS. *Soft music until the attention of the audience is fastened on the picture, then, —*

*Chorus; air, " Soldier's Chorus."*

Glory and fame for the free and bold!
War's red banner let heroes unfold,

Boldly advancing to win renown,
Ay, eager to fight, and ready to guard Rubina's crown.

*Semi-chorus.*

Who lack courage to dare in the front of fight,
With conquest before, and the foe in sight?

*Semi-chorus.*

Who would falter or turn when glory and fame
Their bright laurels press, and with victory bless,
In War's mighty name?

*Chorus.*

Glory and fame, &c.

*Rubina.* Up and away! the tocsin sounds afar;
The land of freedom is the realm of war.

*Repeat chorus, " Glory and Fame," &c., and exit* R.,
RUBINA, *followed by* REVENGE, HATRED, DISCORD,
*and* CRUELTY. *As the music ceases,* QUEEN MAB *and
the* DREAM-SPIRITS *resume their places at back of
bank.*)

*Gloria.* Rubina false, and I, by sleep possessed,
Powerless to rise my rightful crown to wrest!
*Queen Mab.* Now, fair Serena, let thy loyal heart,
The treasures of its secret depths impart.
Sisters, the spell prolong with slumber's chain;
Bind the fair goddess to her dreams again.

*Song:* QUEEN MAB *and* DREAM-SPIRITS; *air,* " *The Image of the Rose.*"

Come, Sleep, on drowsy pinions flying,
    Fair Gloria lull to sweet repose.
The land of dreams around her lying,
    To charm her senses, brightly glows.
There peaceful visions, soft, entrancing,
    In changeful measures sport and play.
Sleep, by thy magic power advancing,
    Within thy arms bear her away.
Magical sleep, bear her, bear her, oh, bear her away!

*As the song proceeds, the* DREAM-SPIRITS *and* QUEEN MAB *slowly exeunt,* R. SERENA, *and* ATTENDANTS, MU-SIC, *with a lyre;* INDUSTRY, *with a distaff;* PLENTY, *with a horn of plenty; and* ART, *with a palette and brushes, — appear,* L., *when the music ceases.* SE-RENA *stands* C., *looking down at* GLORIA ; *her* ATTEND-ANTS L. *The implements carried by the* ATTENDANTS *should be made of flowers, if possible.*

*Bank.*

SERENA.

R.                                          L.

ATTENDANTS.

*Serena.* Genius of Freedom, in thy visions bless
Serena's faithful heart with warm caress.
Let not vain Conquest flatter and deceive :
Bid restful Peace at once thy doubts relieve.
Bending in homage to thy royal sway,
Strong to achieve, and zealous to obey,

13*

She sues for favor : bid her journey wide,
Prosperity to sow on every side.
She pleads in love : receive her earnest prayer,
And of thy love bestow a generous share.

    *Industry.* Hear her, great goddess : ready to inthrall
True-hearted worth, I wait her cheery call.
With brain and muscle ceaselessly I play,
Opening new harvests to the light of day.
Contentment, life's warm, sweet, and better part,
Industry thrones in Labor's thrifty heart.

    *Plenty.* List to her prayer, O Gloria! All elate
To fill the treasure-house of wealth I wait ;
At her command, the harvest shall outpour,
To deck thy chosen land from shore to shore.
Warmed in the love-light of her peaceful eyes,
Plenty, fruit-freighted, shall luxurious rise.

    *Art.* Grant her fond wish, fair goddess, and I twine
Into thy reign, with rare and grand design,
All that pen, brush, and chisel can achieve,
Thy weighty cares to lighten and relieve.
Gigantic Genius bends a willing knee,
When Art, by Peace, to triumph is set free.

    *Music.* Hear her, fair goddess, and I joyous soar,
Pæans of thankfulness and praise to pour
In bounteous song. Thy proud and happy reign
Shall be the burden of my glad refrain.
Religion's anthems swell with large increase
When Music rises at the call of Peace.

    *Serena.* Dost hear, my mistress? All the Graces
      meet
In my behalf, thy favor to entreat.

Grant me thy love, and beautiful and grand
Shall be the labors of this gifted band.


(*Enter* RUBINA, R., *and her* ATTENDANTS.)

*Rubina.* Thou suest for love, Serena, all too late :
Gloria has parted with her high estate.
I sued for power, defied the royal frown,
Played with bold hand, and won the regal crown.
   *Serena.* The crown upon thy head! Oh, bitter woe
O'er a fair land relentlessly shall flow !
Must I relinquish all my dreams of bliss?
Do I deserve such recompense as this?
   *Rubina.* Check thy bold speech, Serena. Get
      thee hence !
Thy piteous pleading is a rash offence
Against our state.
   *Serena.* Rash Rubina, hold !
Peace by thy sway can never be controlled.
Thou hast usurped the guidance of a race
Who shrink in terror from thy brazen face.
Thou hast with treachery obtained a crown ;
Serena quails not at a wicked frown.
Traitress —
   *Rubina.* Defied by thee ! At once away !
Rubina rules, and can relentless slay.
Thy power is crushed : Serena now must cease
The fickle glow of enervating peace.
With all the sprites that compass thee about,
From Freedom's realms I boldly drive thee out.
War's mighty reign begins —

(GLORIA *rises quickly, steps between, and snatches the
    crown from* RUBINA's *head.*)

*Gloria.* False one, 'tis o'er !
Flaunt thy fierce mien in our domain no more.
Thy rude assaults of recklessness and pride,
Fame, glory, and renown, in scorn deride.
Thou hast no charms the noble to inthrall ;
No knightly hearts obey thy martial call
When Conquest beckons. Here, within the realm,
Be thou content to treason overwhelm
With mighty force. Fate binds thee to our side ;
Henceforth thou watchful guard, and we will guide.

(*Waves her hand;* RUBINA *and her* ATTENDANTS *retire
    to back of stage,* L. ; GLORIA *passes behind bank,
    and stands.*)

By vision hath our sleep been girt about,
And happy wake we, free from anxious doubt.
Our choice 'twixt War and Peace we here reveal,
And stamp the fiat with our royal seal.
Approach, Serena ! Love thou dost desire.

(SERENA *stands near* C.)

Thou hast all charms affection to inspire, —
Heart warm with honesty and generous zeal ;
Brain strong to contrive, and mighty to reveal ;
Soul full of teeming virtues. All outflow,
Blessings of peace and love to free bestow.
Henceforth to guide us by thy loving arts,
We crown thee sovereign in our heart of hearts.

*Tableau. The crowning of Peace.*

DREAM-SPIRITS.                    ATTENDANTS.

QUEEN MAB.                        RUBINA.

GLORIA.

*Bank.*

INDUSTRY.          SERENA.          ART.

R. PLENTY.                        MUSIC, L.

SERENA *sits on bank, c., facing audience, hands folded across her breast.* GLORIA *stands behind her, placing the crown upon her head;* INDUSTRY R. *of* SERENA, *seated on bank, facing R., distaff in her left hand resting against shoulder;* ART *in the same position L. of* SERENA, *facing L., with palette in her left hand;* MUSIC *kneeling in front of* ART, *facing audience, playing upon lyre;* PLENTY *kneeling on right knee, front of* INDUSTRY, *outpouring her horn of plenty;* RUBINA L., *back, with her* ATTENDANTS *grouped behind her.* QUEEN MAB *enters R., with her* DREAM-SPIRITS, *and group R., back. Appropriate music: then chorus; air, Eichberg's " National Hymn."*

> On thee, O Freedom, grand and great!
>     In confidence we lean,
> Our land to bless, with fond caress
>     Of happiness serene.
> To hail thy crowning, gentle Peace,
>     Let music joyous soar;
> While harvests wave, and blessings lave
>     Thy realm from shore to shore.

*Repeat.    Curtain.*

Note. — All the tunes used in this allegory, with the single exception of Eichberg's "National Hymn" (which is published in sheet-form), are from "The Grammar School Chorus," which furnished the tunes for "The Revolt of the Bees," "The War of the Roses," and "Lightheart's Pilgrimage," by the same author. Published by O. Ditson & Co., and sold by Lee & Shepard, Boston. Price $1.00.

# THE MERRY CHRISTMAS

OF THE

## OLD WOMAN WHO LIVED IN A SHOE.

# THE MERRY CHRISTMAS

# OLD WOMAN WHO LIVED IN A SHOE.

---

### CHARACTERS.

THE OLD WOMAN who lived in a Shoe.
SANTA CLAUS, disguised as a Beggar.
Ten or twelve CHILDREN, Boys and Girls of various ages.

---

SCENE. — *The exterior of " Copper Toe Shoe House,"*
*which is set at back of platform.*

*Chorus (invisible) ; air, " Revolutionary Tea "* (p. 194,
*" Golden Wreath "* ).

There was an old woman who lived in a shoe;
  Of children she had a score :
So many had she, to know what to do
  Was a question which puzzled her sore.

    (*Head of* CHILD *appears at* 1.)

To some she gave broth without any bread ;
  But never contented were they,
Till she whipped them all soundly, and put them
    to bed,

14                      157

And then very happy were they,
And then very happy were they.

(*Head appears at 2.*)

" Now, mother, dear mother," the young ones
          would cry,
     As they dropped off with a nod,
" To train up a child in the way to go,
     O mother, dear, ne'er spare the rod.

(CHILD's *head appears at 3.*)

For broth without bread is a watery waste;
     And never contented are we,
Till with your good stick it is thickened to taste;

(*Three heads appear at 4.*)

And then, oh, how happy are we!
And then, oh, how happy are we!"

*Enter* OLD WOMAN, R. *Her costume, bodice, quilted
petticoat, sugar-loaf hat, high-heeled shoes, and
cane.*

O. W.   Aha!   (*Heads disappear quick.*)
Good gracious! can't I leave the house a minute,
But what a head's at every window in it?
Don't let me see the tip of a single nose;
For, if you do, we'll surely come to blows.
Poor dears! they want the air.   Well, that is cheap
And strengthening; for they live on air and sleep.
Food is so high, and work is so unstiddy,
Life's really wearing on this poor old widdy.

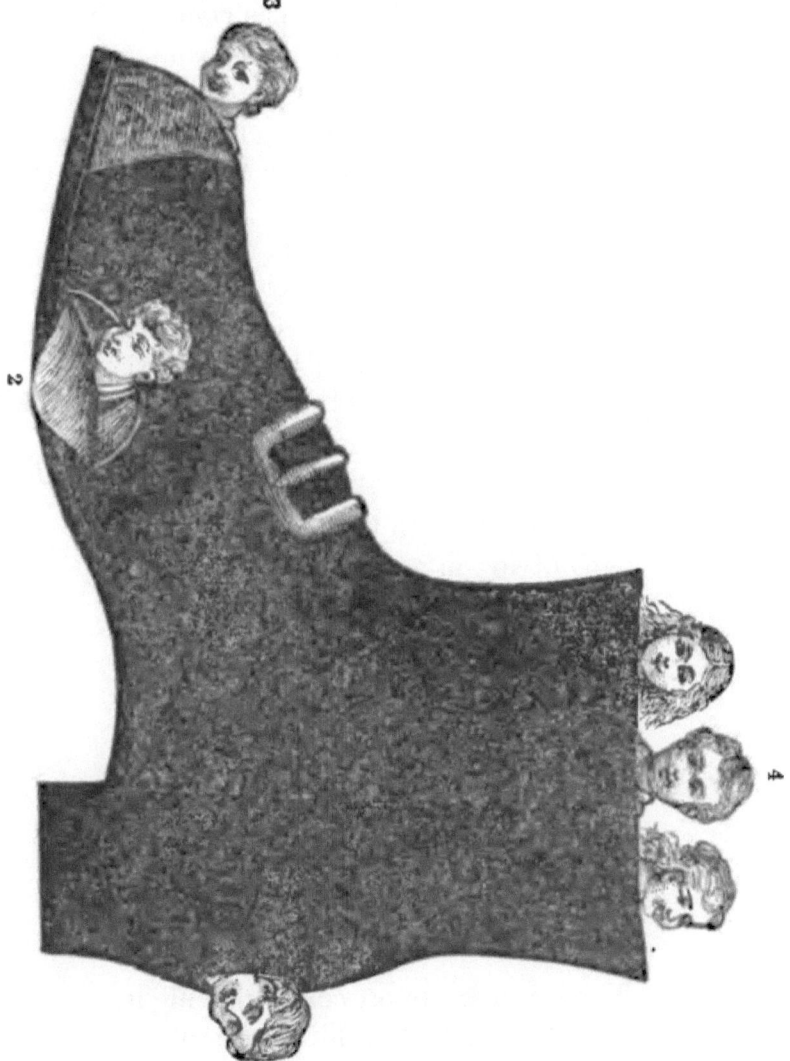

FRONT VIEW OF COPPER TOE SHOE HOUSE.

1. Split in the Heel.
2. Patch on the last Corn.
3. Copper Toe.
4. Lookout, or Observatory at top of House.

(*Heads appear, one after the other, as before.*)

Ah me! here's good old Christmas come again.
How can I join in the triumphant strain
Which moves all hearts?   I am so old and poor,
With none to aid me from their generous store.
    CHILD *at* 1.   Mother, I want a drum.
    CHILD *at* 2.               I want a doll!
    CHILD *at* 3.   Gimme a sword!
    *Three* CHILDREN *at* 4.      Got presents for us all?
    O. W.   Aha!   (*Heads disappear quick.*)
Poor dears! if with the will I had the power,
The choicest Christmas gifts should on them shower.

*Song:* OLD WOMAN; *air,* " *Comin' through the Rye.*"

> If a widdy's with her biddies,
>     Living in a shoe,
> If a widdy's work unstiddies,
>     What'll widdy do?

      (*Heads appear as before.*)

> Every mother loves her biddies;
>     Many a one have I;
> But where get gifts to fill their fists,
>     When I've no gold to buy?

    Aha!   (*Heads disappear quick.*)

> There is a sprite oft comes this night,
>     Whom children love full well;
> But what's his name, and where's his hame,
>     He does not always tell.

*(Heads appear as before.)*

Lads and lassies know good Santa,
 With presents not a few;
Would he were here, my chicks to cheer,
 Living in a shoe!

Aha!   *(Heads disappear.)*
Well, I'll get in, and make the children warm.
Tucked in their beds, they're always safe from harm.
And in their dreams, perhaps, such gifts will rise
As wakeful, wretched poverty denies.

 ·  *(Disappears behind shoe.)*

*Enter cautiously, R., SANTA CLAUS; his fabled dress is
hidden by a long domino, or "waterproof;" he has,
swung about his neck, a tin kitchen, on which he
grinds an imaginary accompaniment to his song.*

*Santa.*   "You'd scarce expect one of my age"—
For gray hair is the symbol of the sage—
To play at "hide-and-seek," to your surprise.
Here's honest Santa Claus, in rough disguise.
But 'tis all right, as I will quick explain,
For I've a mystic project "on the brain."
I've dropped down chimneys all this blessed night,
Where warmth and comfort join to give delight;
I've filled the stockings of the merry elves,
Who, to fond parents, are rich gifts themselves;
And now I've come, resolved to make a show
In that old mansion with the copper toe,
Where dwells a dame, with children great and small,
Enough to stock a school, or crowd a hall.

14*

If they are worthy of our kind regard,
Christmas shall bring to them a rich reward.
So I have donned for once a meaner dress,
To personate a beggar in distress.
If to my wants they lend a listening ear,
The rough old shoe shall glow with Christmas cheer:
If they are rude, and turn me from the door,
Presto! I vanish, and return no more.


*Song:* SANTA CLAUS; *air,* " *Them blessed Roomatics.*"


My name's Johnny Schmoker, and I am no joker;
I don't in my pockets no greenbacks perceive.
For, what with high dressing in fashions distressing,
I can't with a morsel my hunger relieve.
My stomach so tender, that aches there engender;
The whole blessed day I am crying out, "Oh!"
Drat these grand fashions! they wakens my passions,
A-nippin' and gnawin' my poor stomach so!


(*Heads appear as before.*)


I've had the lumbager, dyspepsy, and ager,
With tight-fitting veskits and pantaloons too;
Highsterics and swimins, delirious trimins,
St. Vestris's dance, and the tick dolly-oo.
But not the whole gettin', one's body tight fits in,
Is nottin' to this, which is dretful.   Oh, oh!
Drat these grand fashions! they wakens my passions,
A-nippin' and gnawin' my poor stomach so!

*(Heads disappear.)*

Now, there's a touching song to move the heart,
Hark! what's that?   I thought I heard them start.

*Song:* CHILDREN, *outside; air, " Oh, dear, what can
the matter be ?"*

Oh, dear, what can the matter be?
Dear, dear, what can the matter be?
Oh, dear, what can the matter be?
Somebody's groaning out there !
A hungry old beggar has come here to tease us,
By grinding an organ he knows will not please us.
He hopes it may bring him a handful of pennies,
To buy him a loaf of brown bread.

*Enter* OLD WOMAN, *with* CHILDREN, L.. *from behind
shoe.   The largest hangs on to her skirts, the next
in size to the largest, until they dwindle to the small-
est; repeat song as they enter slowly, turn to* R., 
*march across stage; turn to* L., *march across again;
turn to* R., *and form across stage.*

*O. W.*   Now go away, old man.   'Tis very queer
That you should seek to waste your sweetness here ;
For we've no money, not a cent, to pay
For music ; so you'd better up and move away.
*Santa.*   Alas, alas ! and can you be unkind
To one who's been by Fortune left behind ;
Who has no friend, no money, and no clo'es ;
The hunted victim of unnumbered woes?

Good dame, I ask not money: if you please,
A simple crust my hunger to appease.
    *O. W.* Good gracious! Starving! Children, do
       you hear?
The old man's hungry: quickly disappear!

(CHILDREN *scamper behind shoe.*)

*Santa.* She drives them in. To me 'tis very clear
Old Santa fails to find a welcome here.
    *O. W.* We're very poor, have fasted many a day,
Yet from our door ne'er drove the poor away.

*Song; air, " Balm of Gilead," by the* CHILDREN, *who
march in as before, carrying sticks, on which are
stuck apples, potatoes, crusts of bread, turnip, carrot,
" beat," &c. They move around the stage, singing
as they pass* SANTA; *the last time, pitch their
potatoes, &c., into his tin kitchen. He stands* L. *of
stage;* OLD WOMAN, R.

> Oh, you sha'n't be hungry now,
> Oh, you sha'n't be hungry now,
> Oh, you sha'n't be hungry now,
>     Down at Copper Toe Shoe.
> Cold potato — tato,
> Cold potato — tato,
> Cold pota — to,
>     Down at Copper Toe Shoe.

(*No interlude.*)

Oh, you sha'n't be hungry now,
Oh, you sha'n't be hungry now,
Oh, you sha'n't be hungry now,
    Down at Copper Toe Shoe.
Crusts for breakfast — breakfast,
Crusts for breakfast — breakfast,
Crusts for break — fast,
    Down at Copper Toe Shoe.

Oh, you sha'n't be hungry now,
Oh, you sha'n't be hungry now,
Oh, you sha'n't be hungry now,
    Down at Copper Toe Shoe.
Broth for supper — supper,
Broth for supper — supper,
Broth for sup — per,
    Down at Copper Toe Shoe.

Oh, you sha'n't, &c.

*Santa.* Well, well, I'm puzzled! Here's a grand
    surprise.
Bless me, the tears are dropping from my eyes!
Thank you, my children. This is quite bewitchin';
With eatables you've nearly filled my kitchen.
Ah, little ones! you've learned the better part.
They are the poor who lack the kindly heart;
And they the rich, the noble, and the high,
Who never willing pass the sufferer by.
Now comes my triumph. Children, speak up bright:

What day is this?

    *All.*                Christmas.

    *Little Girl.*              No; 'tis Christmas night!

    *Santa.*  That's true.  Now tell me who, against the laws,

Drops down the chimneys?

    *All.*              Why, old Santa Claus!

    *Santa.*  Bless me! how bright and nice these chil
      dren are!

Each eye doth sparkle like the evening star.

Now, then, suppose I were that ancient sprite,

What would you ask, to give you most delight?

    *Child* 1.  I'd have a sled.

    *Child* 2.          A doll.

    *Child* 3.              A kite for me.

    *Child* 4.  Something still better.

    *Santa.*          What?

    *Child* 4.           A Christmas tree!

    *All Children.*  Oh, my! Good gracious! Wouldn't
      that be grand?

    *O. W.*  Too grand, my chicks, for you to under-
      stand.

Why, such a tree within our old shoe spread,

Would from their fastenings tear out every thread;

Make every peg to start from out its socket,

And send the buckle flying like a rocket.

    *Santa.*  Good, good! there's fun beneath that
      wrinkled phiz.

At playing Santa Claus, let's make a biz.

Suppose me Santa Claus.  I bless you all:

Then from my waistcoat let this oven fall,

*(Takes off kitchen.)*

Throw off this mantle with a sudden jerk,

*(Throws off disguise, and appears as SANTA CLAUS.)*

And in an instant set myself to work.
 *Children.*  'Tis Santa Claus!
 *Santa.*       You're right.  I am the man,
Yours to command.  I'll serve you if I can;
For I have found, good dame, that honest worth
Can burrow in the lowliest spot on earth;
That sweet compassion's ne'er so poorly fed,
But what she finds an extra crust of bread.
Now, to reward your generous hearts, my chicks,
Into the earth these magic seeds I sticks;
These cabalistic words in Hebrew mutter, —
" Ene, mene, moni, suti, sutter;"
Presto! appear! and, glittering bright and free,
Beams on your sight the mystic Christmas tree.

*(Shoe divides, and disappears R. and L.  Curtains at
   back open, disclosing tree.)*

*Song:* "We'll gather round the Christmas Tree."
 SANTA CLAUS *and* OLD WOMAN *distribute presents to
the company.  Curtain falls.*

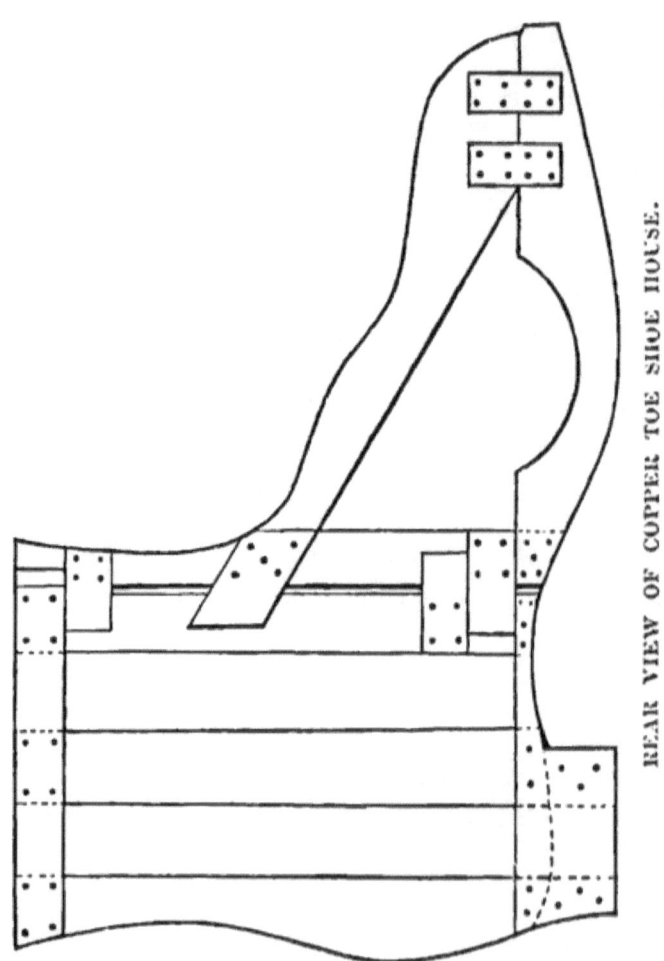

REAR VIEW OF COPPER TOE SHOE HOUSE.

NOTE.—This entertainment was prepared for a Sunday school's Christmas Eve, and was arranged as follows: A stage, fourteen feet square, was fitted with a "roll-up" curtain in front. Drapery was hung at the sides and back; a Christmas tree, filled with presents, was placed well back on the stage, and hidden by curtains arranged to separate in the middle. In front of these was placed "Copper Toe Shoe House." The rear view represents the frame made of wood, in two pieces, to separate in the middle, of the following dimensions: ten feet from toe to heel, five feet and one half from heel to top, four feet and one half across top, heel about twenty inches long, eight inches high. Cover front, in two separate sections, with black cambric; for toe, copper tinsel paper; for sole and patch, brown cambric; for buckle, silver tinsel paper; the patch fastened only at bottom. A curtain, of same material or color as back stage, should be hung in rear of shank, that children standing behind may not be seen. A settee is placed behind it, on which the children in the dwelling stand. 1, 2, and 3 lie upon the stage, and stick their heads out when required. The characters can pass between the curtains at back, to their places. When the tree is disclosed, all the characters are in front, the settee is removed, the braces unfastened, and, at a signal, two boys run off the shoe, and others draw the curtains.

15

# THE

# TOURNAMENT OF IDYLCOURT.

THE TOURNAMENT OF IDYLCOURT.

# THE
# TOURNAMENT OF IDYLCOURT.

## AN ALLEGORY.

---

### CHARACTERS.

JUSTICIA, Genius of Idylcourt.
PRIMEVA, Goddess of Nature.
MAJESTA, Guardian of the Mountains.
LOFTIE, AERIE, Mountain-Spirits.
FLORA, Guardian of the Fields.
POMONA, AGRIA, Field-Spirits.
OCEANA, Guardian of the Sea.
SHELLIE, WAVA, Sea-Spirits.
GENIA, Goddess of Art.
BLENDA, Genius of Painting.
CLASSICA, Genius of Sculpture.
HARMONIA, Genius of Music.
FAITH, HOPE, CHARITY, Classica's Models.
RELIGION, PRAYER, SORROW, JOY, Blenda's Picture.
POESIE, a wandering Maiden.

---

SCENE. — *Idylcourt. For a school exhibition, the chorus should be seated right and left of an open
space in the centre of the platform, for the speakers.
There should be a raised platform, six or eight inches
high, at the rear of this, with a dark background
for the more effective display of tableaux.*

*Opening Chorus; air, "Shady Groves."*

Idylcourt, in fame and beauty
  Glorious, bright thy realms appear;
Idylcourt, in love and duty
  Willing hearts to thee draw near,
  Wise Justicia's words to hear,
  Wise Justicia's words to hear.
Court of genius, home of beauty,
Court of genius, home of beauty,
Court of genius, home of beauty,
  Willing hearts to thee draw near;
Court of genius, home of beauty,
Court of genius, home of beauty,
Court of genius, home of beauty,
  Willing hearts to thee draw near;
Court of genius, love and duty
Render homage to thy beauty,
  Render to thy beauty,
Court of genius, love and duty.

*During the singing of the Chorus, enter,* R., PRIMEVA,
MAJESTA, FLORA, *and* OCEANA. *Enter* L., GENIA,
CLASSICA, BLENDA, HARMONIA. *At the conclusion,
enter* JUSTICIA R., *and stands* C. *Positions are
indicated by the following diagram :—*

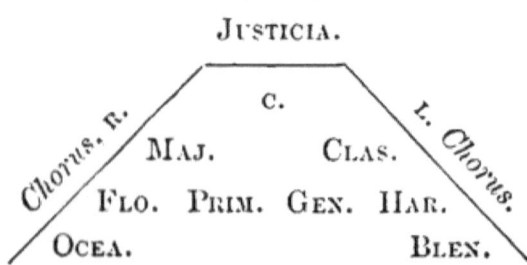

*Justicia.*   Welcome, fair sisters, to our regal court;
Your tuneful measures breathe of good report;
Twin guardian spirits of the fruitful earth,
To glad mankind creation gave you birth.
To you, Primeva, Nature bends in awe;
From you, fair Genia, Art receives its law.
Your free acclaim, upon this regal seat,
Justicia placed, all arguments to meet
With ear impartial; bade her voice decide,
That blissful harmony might here abide.
Your graceful homage, to our royal ear
Is but the foretaste of more welcome cheer.
You need our aid: unto our grateful heart
Your mission's import quickly now impart.
   *Primeva.*   Fair genius —
   *Genia.*                     Sweet Justicia —
   *Justicia.*                                   Our decree,
By courtly rule, admits no double plea.
Be gracious, sisters.
   *Genia.*                  I was wanting grace,
And humbly bend to give Primeva place.
   *Primeva.*   Justicia, yonder proud and haughty
      sprite
Usurps a name Primeva claims by right.
I would have justice!
   *Justicia.*               Art thou just to her?
Genia usurper! 'tis a cruel slur.
Brave, truthful speech bears no envenomed sting,
But, like good metal, has an honest ring.
   *Primeva.*   It was an honest truth. I dare repeat;
I may be rough in speech, but scorn deceit.

*Genia.*  'Tis true, Justicia, in a friendly way,
I chanced to cross Primeva's path to-day,
And held some converse with my sister sprite,
Whose bold, free speech is often my delight.
Our theme was conquest ; and, in pleasant strife,
Each boasted of her power o'er human life ;
And, half in jest, this boast I gayly hurled, —
" I, Genia, am the empress of the world."

*Primeva.*  'Tis false.  It was no jest.
*Justicia.*                    Primeva, cease !
Your angry humor doth disturb our peace.

*Genia.*  Primeva met my jest with frowning
          brow,
And angry words, so bitter in their flow,
My jesting humor fled.  We argued long
To whom, by right, that title should belong ;
Leaving all else but this great truth behind, —
She is the greatest who best serves mankind.

*Justicia.*  Who won the battle?
*Genia.*                    That you must decide.
By your impartial fiat we abide.

*Primeva.*  On this we are agreed.  Justicia, hear,
And let your judgment be both wise and clear.
Nature's own goddess, crowned and sceptred, I
Stand forth all meaner powers to defy.
I rule the field, the mount, the sky, the sea :
Who shall presume in power to rival me?
I wave my hand ; and, o'er the barren waste,
Upspringing flowers to meet my coming haste.
I smile : the trees, o'erburdened with their fruit,
Bend low, with blushing cheeks, for my salute.

I speak : the bristling hillocks, far and near,
Present in homage many an opening ear ;
The grand old mountains, stately and serene,
Welcome my coming, own me as their queen ;
Adown their sides I loose the mimic streams,
To sport and revel in the sun's warm beams.
I rule the mighty sea by wave and tide ;
I deck with starry gems the heavens wide ;
I hurl the storm upon the maddening sea ;
The shifting winds, obedient, follow me ;
I bind the waters in an icy band,
And spread a snowy pall o'er all the land ;
With all the elements I sport at will,
And, fast or loose, all my commands fulfil.
Fair genius, 'tis but just, that, so renowned,
As empress of the world I should be crowned.

    *Justicia.* There's anger in thy speech, pride in
        thine eye ;
Ambition's soaring pinions lift thee high.
What says your rival to this weighty claim?
Can aught be found to heighten Genia's fame?

    *Genia.* Justicia, I a mightier sceptre sway,
And make Primeva's realms but pave the way
To grand achievements. Through her flowery field
I drive the plough, and bounteous harvests yield ;
With skilful husbandry I trim and train,
And bursting garners from wild growth obtain ;
Tunnel her mountains with resistless force,
And make a pathway for the iron horse ;
Gird up her waters to obey my will,
And move the strong arm of the whirring mill.

Across her broad expanse, the mighty sea,
My white-winged messengers move swift and free;
From out their earthen graves I pluck the gems
That warm and shape, or glow in diadems.
In aërial flights I wander through her sphere,
Or with rare science draw her planets near,
With touch electric feel the farthest clime,
And count the storm-specks on the wings of time.
She empress of the world! it cannot be;
All her possessions minister to me.
Rough and ill-shaped the treasure she displays;
I mould and carve, and make the jewel blaze.
I claim the crown.   Justicia, be thou true;
She must be greatest who can all subdue.

> *Justicia.*   Unto this haughty speech, and fulsome
>     praise,
We've listened. Genia, in a wild amaze.
Hast thou forgot, self-laudatory boast
Was ne'er the leader of a conquering host?
But that to sober justice we're allied,
We should be merry at such foolish pride.

> *Genia.*   We wait your verdict.
> *Primeva.*                   'Twill give me the crown.
> *Genia.*   Primeva, cease.
> *Primeva.*                   I care not for your frown.
Betwixt the false and true she *must* decide:
Mine is the wise, and yours the foolish pride.

> *Justicia.*   This idle skirmish doth our court defame;
A silly quarrel for an empty name.

> *Primeva.*   A silly quarrel! Is Justicia fair,
To shun a verdict by excuse so bare?

*Genia.*   She's bound to rule whene'er we make
    appeal :
Be wise, Justicia, and your choice reveal.
    *Justicia.*   Hear, then, the judgment which we now
    proclaim : —
As each has sought to blazon her own fame,
The key to right in this one truth we find, —
She is the greatest who best serves mankind.
On this you are agreed.   Here rest your case,
And leave the verdict to the human race.
Ofttimes, in Idylcourt, you've chanced to meet
An earthly maid, who favors our retreat,
With curious, watchful eyes, as though she sought
Food for the nourishment of new-born thought, —
A goodly type of fair, ingenuous youth,
About whom floats an atmosphere of truth.
Woo her, fair sisters, with all fair device,
Which should in honest rivalry suffice ;
In peaceful tourney meet to win the maid ;
And on the victor shall our hand be laid
In benediction of so wise a choice ;
Then harmony prevails, and all rejoice.
    *Primeva.*   An admirable plan.
    *Genia.*                     Justicia's right.
    *Justicia.*   Prepare your forces for the bloodless fight.
Be earnest in the strife, but loyal ever,
And some success *must* crown a right endeavor.

      *Chorus; air, " New-mown Hay."*

      Then gayly to the tourney hie,
        And struggle for the crown ;

The strong in right shall all defy,
The wrong in shame go down.
In peaceful contest meeting,
All courteous be the greeting.
We arm, the contest to begin :
Hurrah! the right shall win!

*At the words, "All courteous," JUSTICIA extends her right hand; PRIMEVA lays her left hand upon it; GENIA lays her right. They stand thus until the chorus ends. Then repeat the chorus. JUSTICIA steps back, and exit R.; PRIMEVA and GENIA with their attendants countermarch, and exeunt R. and L. As the song ceases, enter from R., POESIE.*

*Poesie.* Vanquished again! Was ever mortal maid
By wild, illusive phatoms so betrayed?
Taught by a wise old seer that Idylcourt
Of guiding genii is the famed resort,
I've wandered in and out for weary hours,
Seeking the leaders of those mighty powers
That robe the earth in beauty, seasons guide,
Hang out the stars, and shift the changing tide,
Endow with action all the sons of earth,
And to the good and beautiful give birth.
Alas! my search is vain. About me glide
Tormenting shadows, that my calls deride.
I feel their presence in the fragrant breeze ;
I touch their fingers in the fruited trees ;
I spy their images in mirrored fount ;
I hear their music in the echoing mount.

I know that at their touch fair cities rise ;
That at their call delighted progress flies ;
That at their smiles e'en towering genius soars
To loftier heights, and richer spoil secures.
And yet far off they stand.   I cannot meet
The love-light of their eyes, or at their feet
Drink in the wisdom of inspiring speech.
The springs of power rise far beyond my reach.
Hear me, ye spirits, wonderful and grand !
Upon your charmèd ground I fearless stand.
Come ye in frightful shapes, or forms of grace,
I challenge you to meet me face to face.

*Chorus:* " *The Fairy's Revel.*"

The mountains are sending their forces in might ;
The fields are upspringing, and girding for fight ;
The sea is outpouring, the air is alive,
For thee, fair Primeva, in tourney to strive.

*During which, enter, R.,* PRIMEVA ; FLORA, *bearing
    flowers;* POMONA, *bearing basket of fruit;* AGRIA,
    *with a bundle of dried grass, hay, and grain;*
    OCEANA, SHELLIE, WAVA, MAJESTA, LOFTIE, AERIE,
    *and take positions according to following diagram :—*

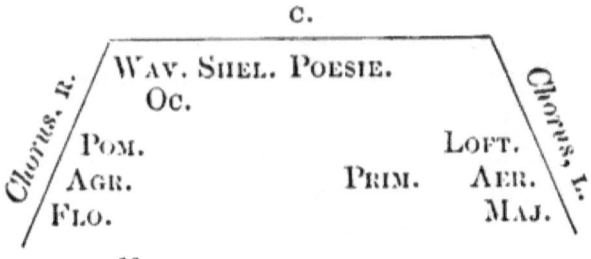

16

*Poesie.*   Conquered at last; and yet with strange
    affright
I am possessed at this most dazzling sight.
Fair spirits, at my call you've kindly met.
I'm little skilled in your court etiquette:
Accept the homage of a grateful heart,         ·
That long will cherish what you may impart.
  *Primeva.*   A suitor for that heart behold in me, —
Primeva, Nature's goddess, strong and free.
Follow my footsteps, and the path of life
Shall be with beauty and instruction rife.
Nature's grand empire all inviting opes,
To crown with joy and bliss thy youthful hopes.
The realm of matter owns my sovereign sway;
All working forces my commands obey.
But give to me thy heart, and onward press,
For I've the power to beautify and bless.
Come thou, fair Flora, guardian of my fields,
Display the charms thy rich dominion yields.


(FLORA *steps upon platform at* L. *of* POESIE.   POMONA
    *and* AGRIA *step behind them.*)


  *Flora.*   Broad and bright, in beauty and in worth,
The realms I govern stretch about the earth:
In pastures where the meek-eyed cattle graze,
In clustering woodlands, musical with praise,
In mighty forests where the untamed rove,
O'er rich plantations, through the tropic grove,
O'er plain and prairie, noiseless to the tread,
My regal green luxuriously is spread.

Out of my thrifty soil mankind's supplies,
At lusty labor's call, obedient rise.
With fancy's touch I skilfully combine
Grove, hill, and river in a rare design,
And spread for Genius, rich, attractive views
She fails to catch, yet hopefully pursues.
Come to my realms, fair maid! Primeva's heart
With warmest love shall purest joys impart.

 *Agria.* Haste, gentle maid, into our fair retreat:
Agria will lay her treasures at thy feet.

 *Pomona.* And in thy lap, from her abundant store,
Pomona will her choicest treasures pour.

 *Flora.* Thou shalt be welcomed with a matchless
   song,   .
Our heaven-taught singers joyously prolong;
On mossy beds recline for happy hours,
Charmed by rich perfumes, decked with lovely flowers.

*Tableau : " Flora's Tribute."  Music.*

POESIE *sinks on one knee, making a "lap" of her
dress with her hand.* FLORA *steps behind, holding
flowers over her head.* AGRIA *at* R., *kneeling, in
the act of laying her treasures at her feet.* POMONA,
L., *bending forward, about to pour her fruits into
her lap.* OCEANA *with her arms about* WAVA *and*
SHELLIE, R. *and* L., *kneel.* MAJESTA, LOFTIE, *and*
AERIE *form a standing group, with arms thrown
about each other.* POMONA *passes to back,* L. *corner.*
FLORA *looks down at* POESIE. POESIE *has her head
thrown back, looking up at* FLORA. *All the others
look at* POESIE. *Music continues until the group is
well settled in position, then, —*

*Chorus; air, " The First Violets."*

Come with gentle Flora, fair fields to rove.
She can deck with beauty, she will share with love.
Bathed by the sunlight, and fed by the dew,
Her bright and verdant regions are opening to you.

*Poesie (springing to her feet; others retiring to their
first positions).*

Sweet, gentle Flora, take me to your heart;
In all your joys I long to bear a part.
  *Primeva.* Nay, not so fast, fair maiden. List again.
Majesta burns your homage to obtain ;
She is the guardian of the mountains high,
Whose peaks in grandeur pierce the arching sky.
  *Majesta.*  Where the fierce eagle builds her dizzy
      nest,
Amid the clouds, I take my regal rest.
The sun on me his morning kiss bestows,
And nightly wraps me in his farewell glows.
The storm-king grimly musters round my throne,
And sends his chariots to the farthest zone.
My realms stretch far and wide o'er all the land,
And monuments of awe-inspiring grandeur stand.
Within my treasure-caverns locked secure,
Are precious stones, and veins of gleaming ore ;
Marbles and granites — sleeping giants — lie,
Long to escape the crafty builder's eye.
Come to my realm, fair maid, and thou shalt find
The golden talisman that lures mankind.
From towering summits watch the creeping world ;
See beauty's colors gloriously unfurled ;

Hear the weird echoes bound from steep to steep;
And see the lightning take his earthward leap.
Primeva's fortress shall thy guardian be:
Give me thy hand, and upward mount with me.

*Tableau: " The Listeners." Music.*

MAJESTA *stands* c., *with left hand pointing up over
audience.* POESIE, *kneeling* R., *places her left hand
in* MAJESTA'S *left, and bends forward, intently gazing
in the direction in which she points, her right hand
behind her ear.* LOFTIE *passes to* L. *of* MAJESTA,
*and kneels with her hand on the waist of* MAJESTA.
AERIE *in same position,* R. *of* POESIE. OCEANA *and
her sprites form a standing group,* R., *back.* PRIME-
VA *steps back of all; and* FLORA *and her sprites form
standing group,* L., *back. Music continues until all
arranged, then,* —

*Chorus; air, " The Herd-Bells."*
Amid the mountains fleeting,
    The echoes linger long,
Earth's song of praise repeating,
    In chorus rich and strong.
The grand old mountains proudly
    Their heads in beauty raise,
And, bathed in blushing glory,
    Accept the song of praise.

[*The effect could be heightened by concealing a chorus
at the farther end of the hall, and introducing an
echo refrain in the song.*]
16*

*Poesie (springing up; the others resuming their former positions).*

Upward, Majesta, guide my willing feet;
I long to share the joys of your retreat.
 *Primera.*  Curb your impatience once again, I
  crave.
Speak, Oceana, guardian of the wave.
 *Oceana.*  Know me, fair maid, as guardian of
  the sea,
The wealth of waters stretching far and free,
Deep basined in the world; in peace as mild,
As bright and beauteous, as a sportive child;
Dancing in sunlight up and down the sand;
Leaping, with white-capped waves, the rocky strand;
Creeping to shady nooks on pebbly bed;
Sleeping in moonlight 'neath a silvery spread.
Over her rolling roads, in strength and pride,
The floating treasure-chests of nations glide;
In emerald pastures deep beneath her crest,
The fin-clad wanderers from their gambols rest.
At mankind's call she hastes to do her part,
And from her herds bestows with generous heart.
Far, far below, fair cities rear their walls
With jewelled keeps, and coral-caverned halls.
Come to my realms, fair maid, and float with me
Upon the bosom of the swelling sea.
Hark to the song of Naiads far below;
See in the sunlight yonder billows glow.

*Tableau: " The Gazers."   Music.*

OCEANA *kneels on one knee* R. *of* POESIE, *pointing off*
R.   POESIE *places her left hand on* OCEANA'S *shoulder, leans forward, shades her eyes with right hand,
and looks in the direction of pointed hand.* SHELLIE
*comes* L. *of* POESIE, *a little behind her, and kneels
quickly, holding a shell in her hand.* WAVA *kneels
in front of all, with her finger to her lip, and her
hand waving silence to* PRIMEVA, *who stands* L.
AERIE *and her sprites form a standing group,* L.,
*back, and* MAJESTA *and her sprites the same,* R.,
*back; all looking in the direction in which* OCEANA
*points.   Music continues until the picture is complete,
then, —*

*Chorus; air, " Boating Song."*

Gayly, ye billows, among you we play ;
Take us up gently, and bear us away ;
Light on the surface of ocean we glide ;
Deep in her bosom we fearless abide.
Roving at pleasure, joyous and free,
Rocked in the arms of the murmuring sea.

*Poesie (starting up; others resume former positions).*

Among thy happy scenes I long to roam ;
Bright Oceana, take me to thy home.
     *Primeva.*   Thou shalt be free to roam field, mount,
          and sea,
If thou but give thy gentle heart to me.
These sisters three, my ministers of state,
My edicts to enforce, obedient wait ;

And I, submissive to a heavenly will,
With mighty powers its commands fulfil.
I own no earthly rule, no rival fear;
Beauty and grandeur at my voice appear;
What title, Poesie, will you here bestow
On one in whom such rare endowments glow?

*Poesie.* Thy glorious visions wrap me in amaze;
Speech were too poor, in eloquence of praise,
To frame a title that would fitly stand
To mark a power so wonderful and grand.
What title can I give? I pray thee tell.

*Primeva.* The empress of the world would suit me
well.

### *Enter* JUSTICIA, R.

*Justicia.* Hold, rash Primeva! not to gain applause
Should wild ambition overstep our laws. —
What thou hast heard, fair mortal, ponder long,
For hasty action often strengthens wrong;
Another suitor comes; give willing ear:
Weigh well all doubts; then let the truth appear.

[*Exit*, R.

### *Chorus:* "*The Fairy's Revel.*"

The armies of Genius outpour in their might,
Fair Science is marching her clans to the fight.
At the call of its mistress Art's realms are alive,
For thee, lovely Genia, in tourney to strive.

(*During the chorus, all upon the platform move round
back of* POESIE, *and form in line. Enter* L. GENIA,
BLENDA, *and* CLASSICA.)

*Poesie.*  Another brilliant throng, so fair and bright,
My spirit quickens with a new delight.
Welcome, sweet friends : if me you come to greet,
Such glowing honors lay me at your feet.
  *Genia.*  Kneel not to me ; I come to win thy heart.
The suitor here should choose the lowly part.
Fair mortal, listen.  Genia is my name :
Art's chosen goddess, mighty is my fame.
Thou art the offspring of that sovereign Thought,
Under whose sway the universe is brought ;
And I, the guiding genius of mankind,
In bonds submissive, Nature's realms to bind.
Before my birth, the world was filled with strife,
And all the squalor of barbaric life ;
The human race in ignorance sunk deep,
Content to live and die in sloth and sleep.
But, with my coming, energy awoke,
And reason through the deadening chaos broke ;
Awakened Thought, in wonder, sought by lore
Creation's mystic riddle to explore ;
And, as she strove, the world's great change was
        wrought,
With purer joys from deeper delvings brought.
Beneath my sway, all's wonderful and grand
Where taste and culture deck what Nature planned.
Give me thy heart. and with all-conquering might
'I'll guide thy steps through life to realms of light.
I bring three sisters in my regal train,
Who high in Art's supreme dominion reign. —
Blenda, approach.  Thy skill to Poesie show,
And let rare colors on thy canvas glow.

*Blenda.* In Nature's studio, Blenda's models rise
In various shapes to gladden and surprise.
The shadows of their beauties to secure,
Leads genius many trials to endure.
But what a triumph waits the earnest heart,
Who on the canvas sees her trophies start
To life and action, adding, age on age,
To history many a bright, illumined page!
Portraying vice with rarely gifted hand,
She sees a warning light 'gainst passion stand.
Depicting virtue in her pure attire,
She warms all hearts to worship and aspire.
Inwrapping sense and soul with pleasure high,
To homage leads the world's applauding cry.
Look on the picture I will now display, —
Religion standing in the heavenly way,
Her finger pointing in the Book of truth,
Instruction pouring in the ears of youth.

*Tableau: " The Heavenly Way." Music.*

BLENDA *takes* POESIE'S *hand, and leads her* R., *then
turns, and points to* C. POESIE *falls upon her knees
with clasped hands.* PRIMEVA *and her sprites, who
are in a line, back, separate* R. *and* L., *disclosing
group.* RELIGION, *standing* C., *an open Bible sup-
ported on her left hand, rests upon her arm, the open
pages towards audience; her right hand rests on the
page, with one finger pointing. At her right hand,
kneels* JOY, *pointing with her left hand to* RELIGION,
*her right on the shoulder of* SORROW, *who is crouch-
ing before her, with her face buried in her hands.*

*Left of* RELIGION, PRAYER *kneels, joining the hands
of a little child who is in front of her: she is looking
up at* RELIGION. *Music soft and low, until the
group is formed, then,* —

*Chorus: " How gently, how calmly."*

So gently, so calmly descending,
Religion glides over the earth,
  So pure, so bright,
She decks the earth with heavenly light,
That charms to calm and sweet repose.
  Oh, lovely spirit!
Genia in triumph shall soon arise;
Blenda calls beauty from out the skies;
She shall be honored evermore;
Goddess of Art, your crown is secure.
  Joyous are we, &c.

*(Music continues until all change to their old positions.)*

*Poesie.*  I am enraptured with your beauteous art;
Sweet Blenda, let me henceforth share your heart.
 *Genia.*  Classica waits, fair maid: we hold her
  dear;
With words of counsel let her now draw near.
 *Classica.*  Dull, senseless stone, I train to living
  grace,
Trace beauty's lines upon the pallid face;
From sullen marble draw the prisoned heart,
And strength and sense to meaner clay impart.
Over the earth I rear the grandest homes,
With towering pinnacles, and stately domes;

While tombs and pyramids for ages stand,
To mark the workings of my gifted hand.
Who follows me must labor hard and long,
Be brave in trial, and in patience strong.
The tasks I spread, by perils oft beset,
The sculptor strengthen, when courageous met;
Through me, life-studies he must ponder o'er,
And dive deep down in streams of classic lore;
And, if he fails to reach his ideal plan,
Out of his struggles he has carved — a man.
But, if he triumphs, grand is his renown;
Fame can bestow no more enduring crown.
Upon my marbles, maiden, look with me;
Faith, Hope, and Charity, — the peerless three.

*Tableau: " The Peerless Three."    Music.*

CLASSICA *takes* POESIE'S *hand, and leads her* R., *then
turns, and points* C. POESIE *falls upon her knees.
The characters at back separate, showing group:*
CHARITY, *a tall figure,* C., *her left hand upon the
left shoulder of a child, who stands nearly in front
of her, half turned towards her, with outstretched
hand, into which* CHARITY *is in the act of dropping a
coin, with her right hand. At* R. *of* CHARITY *stands*
HOPE, *leaning upon an anchor, looking at* CHARITY.
*On her* L. *stands* FAITH, *with her arms folded about
a large cross, which rests upon the platform, and
reaches above her shoulder.* FAITH *and* HOPE *should
be a little shorter than* CHARITY. *All the figures in
plain white, no colors; the cross and the anchor
should be white. Music soft and low until all is
arranged, then, —*

*Chorus; air, " How gently, how calmly."*

How calmly, how sweetly relieving,
Moves Charity over the earth,
    With Faith and Hope!
They deck the earth with heavenly light,
That charms to calm and sweet belief.
    Oh, lovely spirits!
Genia in triumph shall now arise;
Classica calls from out the skies;
Her works for ages shall endure;
Goddess of Art, your crown is secure.
    Joyous are we, &c.

*Poesie (starting up; line at back changing as
before).*

Classica, thy sculptured forms are all divine.
Has Art another realm can equal thine?
  *Genia.* Thou shalt be judge, fair maid; within my
    train,
Is one who can the wildest heart enchain;
She rules the realm of song, melodious moves,
Gathering the warbled sweets of woodland groves;
And thence distilling soul-entrancing lays,
That fill the earth with peace, the heavens with praise.
Spirit of music. sweet Harmonia, wake:
Of thy rich gifts bid Poesie partake.

*Music. Characters at back separate.* HARMONIA *discovered,* c., *standing erect, a lyre in her left hand,
the fingers of her right upon the strings.* POESIE
*moves up, and kneels at her feet, looking up at her*
17

*with clasped hands.   The characters group themselves
in sitting and reclining positions about her.   PRIMEVA
and GENIA stand at extreme R. and L., back.*

*Solo and chorus: " So merrily over the Ocean
Spray."*

HARMONIA *sings the three solos, then full chorus.*

*Solo.*   I am queen of the realm of song,
  My home the harmonious sea,
Where the spirits of music prolong
  Unceasing a welcome for me.
From the song wave they merrily brave,
  Melodious voices glide ;
Oh, sweet is their song as it floateth along
  The crest of the tremulous tide !

*Chorus.*   So merrily over the sea of song,
  Rising and falling we float along ;
So merrily over the sea of song,
  Gayly we float along.
  Gayly over the sea,
  Harmonia's spirits free,
    Singing, singing,
  Happy, happy are we.
As merrily over the sea of song,
Rising and falling we float along ;
So merrily over the sea of song,
  Over the sea of song,
  Gayly we float along,
  Gayly we float along.

(*When the song is ended, all keep their places, POESIE
kneeling, with her eyes fixed upon HARMONIA. A
pause; then GENIA steps to the side of POESIE.*)

*Genia.* Silent, fair Poesie? What! no words of praise
As tribute to Harmonia's matchless lays?
*Poesie.* Can words pay fitting homage to her art?
My tribute's here, in this high-swelling heart,
Which, filled with rapture, checks the flow of speech
That would aspire to praise it cannot reach.
*Genia.* And so I triumph. Maiden, unto me
This soaring spirit bends the humble knee ;
Is but a slave to work my sovereign will,
And with her sisters my commands fulfil.
Over the earth unnumbered spirits bind,
At smile from me, rich blessings for mankind ;
What title can she claim who thus displays
All that can bless and strengthen and amaze?
*Poesie.* What title can she claim? You ask *me* this,
Whose soul is filled with one rich draught of bliss, —
Harmonia's mistress?
*Genia.*                    I that spirit claim.
*Primeva* (*comes down* L. POESIE *rises*).
'Tis false! 'Twas I, Primeva, gave her fame.
From heaven she came, to purify and bless ;
And Nature nurtured her with warm caress.
*Genia.* 'Twas Art's rich culture trained her infant
            voice
In grand, majestic numbers to rejoice.
*Primeva.* Genia, no more ; let Poesie decide
Upon our claims. Her judgment we abide.
*Genia.* I am content.

*Poesie.*   Of me, ye judgment seek?
You, strong and mighty, I but poor and weak.
   *Primeva.*   To save a sovereign title of command,
Nature and Art in strife before you stand.
In full accord our forces are combined
For this great task,—to serve and bless mankind.
Who is the greatest?   Fearlessly proclaim.
We ask your verdict in Justicia's name.
Both have our powers skilfully unfurled;
Who shall be crowned as empress of the world?
   *Poesie.*   O spirits regal, beautiful, and wise!
In unity supreme your glory lies;
Can frail mortality presume to call
Her judgment forth, to make you rise or fall?
Fair Genia, through your realms of thought and light,
I wander in a maze of grand delight;
Behold mankind upspring in strength and grace,
And sturdy tasks courageously embrace.
As through your realms, Primeva, free I rove,
My spirit glows with reverence and love.
I see your earth, so wonderful and vast,
Which proud man conquers, conquer him at last;
And in both Art and Nature see the hand
Which wields the sceptre of supreme command,
Where each within my heart holds equal place,
I could not elevate, would not abase.

(*Joins their hands.*)

Together reign, and teach mankind the way
To that grand realm, and that one sovereign sway.

*Enter* JUSTICIA, C.

*Justicia.*    A righteous verdict, which we joyous seal.
Our tourney's ended : let the chorus peal.

*Tableau :* JUSTICIA *on platform, with her hands raised
in benediction over* POESIE, *who stands before her,
joining the hands of* GENIA, L., *and* PRIMEVA, R. ;
GENIA's *followers on her* L., PRIMEVA's *followers on
her* R.

*Chorus, same as opening chorus.*

Idylcourt, in love and beauty, &c.

(*Curtain.*)

NOTE. — The airs, "Shady Groves," and "Boatman's Song,"
can be found in "The Grammar School Chorus." The other
airs are from the new "Fourth Music Reader," published by
Ginn Brothers.  Price, $1.50.  Furnished by Lee and Shepard,
Boston.
17*

# A THORN AMONG THE ROSES.

# A THORN AMONG THE ROSES.

---

## CHARACTERS.

MRS. CANDOR, Principal of Rosebush Institute.
PATIENCE PLUNKETT, the oldest of her pupils, age thirty-five.
LUCY WOODS,
BESSIE TRAVERS,
JANE TURNER, } Pupils.
AUGUSTA STEPHENS,
MARIA MELLISH,
BRIDGET MAHONY, the cook, age fifty.
TOM CANDOR, MRS. CANDOR'S nephew, a homesick youth of nineteen.
JOB SEEDLING, lad-of-all-work, age twenty.

---

## COSTUMES.

PATIENCE PLUNKETT. A very girlish attire, with an old face strongly marked; red hair, with corkscrew ringlets.
JOB SEEDLING. Dark pants, rather short, white jacket, apron, stockings and shoes.
Other characters appropriately dressed.

---

SCENE. — *Music-room at Rosebush Institute; piano, back, c. ; lounge or sofa, L. ; arm-chair, R. ; two or three chairs, R. and L. Entrance from R.*

201

(*Enter* Bessie Travers *and* Lucy Woods.)

*Bessie.*   Madam Solfa has really gone off in a pet?

*Lucy.*   Yes: because poor me could not run up the musical scale with celerity, — in fact, stuck fast at the bottom, — her highness complained to Mrs. Candor; and Mrs. Candor — bless her! — took my part.   "If the poor child cannot sing, let her alone." — "But se most be made to seeng," says madam; "and se weel steek to 'do,' and go no furzer." — "Well, let her stick there, if she likes.   Her father's a baker, and she has a perfect right to stick to dough, if she likes it."   So madam, shocked at the levity of our delightful preceptress, put on her bonnet and shawl, and vanished in a blaze of fury.

*Bessie.*   O Lucy, you have driven the poor lady away!

*Lucy.*   But she won't be gone long, depend upon it; for she left her baggage behind, and there's a quarter's salary due her.

*Bessie.*   And we must go without our lesson to-day.

*Lucy.*   I'm glad of it.   There's no music in my soul.   I must be " fit for treason and conspiracies."

*Bessie.*   You are the smartest girl in the school, Lucy, with this *inharmonious* exception.

*Lucy.*   I the smartest?   You flatter me; and you forget our aged schoolmate, Patience Plunkett.

*Bessie.*   Aged!   Why, Lucy, what could have possessed that mature — to speak mildly — female to class herself with young girls like us?

*Lucy.*   I'm sure I don't know; but Maria Mellish,

who is always fishing out mysteries, told me her father,
a farmer, has recently made a mint of money; and
Patience has a foolish idea that she can procure an
education, even at her age, and so entered Rosebush
Institute as a pupil.

*Bessie.*  Poor thing! she is the laughing-stock of
the school, and cannot be made to see it.

*Lucy.*  She has one devoted admirer, Job Seedling.
The silly gander is evidently in love, and takes no
pains to conceal it.  At the table he forgets his occupation, and stands staring at her.

*Bessie.*  She certainly receives a great deal of
attention, and all the tidbits, there.  (*Enter* MARIA
MELLISH, R.)

*Maria.*  O girls! I have found it out at last.
Only think of it! a romance in Rosebush Institute!
Yes: now, don't speak of this, — Job Seedling, the
meek, patient Job, is a prince in disguise.

*Bessie.*  A prince? Nonsense.

*Maria.*  Well, not exactly a prince; but Hopps the
milkman told me that Johnson the butcher told him
that Bates the expressman told him that Patience
Plunkett belongs in Razorly, and that his agent there
told him that Job Seedling was the son of a rich farmer; that he got desperately enamoured of Patience,
and followed her here, taking a menial situation that
he might be near the object of his love.  Isn't it
splendid?

*Lucy.*  Splendid.  If Mrs. Candor should hear of
this, I fear that Job would have to give up his menial
situation for a meaner.

*Maria.* But nobody shall tell her. I mean to watch them. It will be such fun to hear Job sigh as he passes the butter, see him roll his eyes as he lifts the rolls. Oh, it's just jolly! (*Enter* JANE TURNER *and* AUGUSTA STEPHENS.)

*Jane.* O girls! have you heard the news? Tom —

*Augusta.* Candor has just arrived.

*Jane.* Sick. Only think of it! Come here to be nursed. And he looks awfully.

*Augusta.* Mrs. Candor hurried him off to bed at once, ordered hot jugs for his feet, hot ginger-tea, and a cold towel for his head.

*Maria.* Dear me! and I never heard a word of it!

*Lucy.* He ought to have a holiday, and go home.

*Maria.* Oh, wouldn't that be fun! Poor fellow! I'm so sorry for him! But then, he can have jam, and jellies, and all the consolations of sickness. I think it's rather pleasant to be sick — a little. (*Enter* MRS. CANDOR, *equipped for going out.*)

*Mrs. Candor.* Girls, I must run down and see Dr. Bruce.

| | |
|---|---|
| *Augusta.* ⎫ | Is he very sick? |
| *Maria.* ⎬ (*Together.*) | Is he going to die? |
| *Lucy.* ⎭ | Is he dangerous? |

*Mrs. Candor.* I hope not.

| | |
|---|---|
| *Augusta.* ⎫ | Will school close? |
| *Maria.* ⎬ (*Together.*) | Shall we have a holiday? |
| *Lucy.* ⎭ | Will you send us home? |

*Mrs. Candor.* Dear me, what talkers! Keep quiet, girls. I'll run down and tell the doctor his symptoms.

*Bessie.* Let me go for him, Mrs. Candor.

*Other girls (in chorus).* Let me! I'll go! We'll all go! Do let us go!

*Mrs. Candor.* No: I don't want to have him come unless it is necessary. He can determine that when I tell him the symptoms. So keep quiet. There will be no music-lesson, and you can amuse yourselves until my return — under the rules, remember. Dear me! what could have sent that boy home sick? [*Exit.*

*Maria.* Amuse ourselves! Oh, isn't that nice? Let's have a game of tag!

*Augusta.* Nonsense! With that poor sick youth over our heads?

*Maria.* That's so! We must be quiet. (*Enter* BRIDGET.)

*Bridget.* If yez plase, ma'am, what'll I do? Shure, the misthress is nowhere at all, at all.

*Bessie.* No, Bridget: she's gone to the doctor's.

*Bridget.* To the doctor's, is it? 'Pon my sowl, there's throuble be comin' to the place. Didn't I say a windin'-sheet in the flame av me candle last night? Shure, that's a sign av disolation.

*Bessie.* It's a sign the candle wanted snuffing, Bridget.

*Bridget.* Oh, be dacent, Miss Bessie! Don't make light av the signs. Shure, I seed it in a candle onct whin me brither Pathrick was ailin' wid the masles, and jist fourteen months and six days from that very night he died.

*Maria.* Of the measles?

*Bridget.* Go long wid yez! Didn't he fall into a well, and break his neck wid drowning?

18

*Augusta.* Now, Bridget, Mrs. Candor told us we might amuse ourselves while she is gone. Do you know what would *most* amuse us?

*Bridget.* Troth, I don't.

*Augusta.* A nice mince-pie.

*Maria.* Oh, yes; and some cold tongue!

*June.* And a pickle. Don't forget a pickle.

*Bridget.* I'll forgit meself if I git any sich dilicases. No, no: I'll not be afther givin' yez ony sich divar-shun.

*Maria.* O Bridget! you know me. I've got an elegant breastpin, that will look well —

*Augusta.* Fastened to a pretty green necktie that I've no use for.

*June.* And they will match a nice pair of earrings that mother has promised to send me for somebody — you know, Bridget.

*Bridget.* Och, the darlints! It's the foine wheedlin' way yez have, onyhow. Well, well, it's meself will look into the panthry; an' if there's a *delicate* morsel, that's in danger av shpoiling, mayhap it moight find its way up here. But I'll make no promises.

[*Exit.*

*Maria.* Now let's have a dance.

*Augusta.* Oh, that's splendid! (*Enter* PATIENCE.)

*Patience.* A dance! A dance in the halls of learning! Horrible! Girls, it must not be! You shock me. *I* came here to cultivate my understanding.

*Maria.* And dancing will do it, Patience: it's just the thing for the understanding.

*Patience.* Maria Mellish, I'm ashamed of you. You want polish.

*Maria.* A polished floor is delightful, but not necessary to the poetry of motion. Come, girls, a dance, a dance!

*Patience.* Not in my presence. I will be no spec-*takor* of such priv-priv — nonsense. No: we are here for a higher purpose; to enlarge our ca-ca — talents, to store our minds with the in-in — things which the great minds of all ages have con-con — got together for good.

*Maria (aside to* AUGUSTA). Poor Patience! how she trips at the hard words!

*Patience.* If there is any dancing here, I shall feel under ob-ob — I shall tell Mrs. Candor.

*Maria.* Well, Miss Tattler, you shall be under no ob-ob to do any such thing, for we won't dance.

*Patience.* If we have a leisure hour, it cannot be better employed than in the per-per — reading of a useful book.

*Maria.* That's so. (*Goes to* R., *and calls.*) Here, Job, bring Miss Patience the dictionary. Come, girls, let's have a sing.

*Augusta (aside to* MARIA). Hateful old thing!

*Bessie.* Let us look over the music; perhaps we can find something sweet and soft, that will not disturb the invalid.

*Jane.* Good! "Mulligan Guards," or, "Gentle Spring." (*They go to the piano, which should be placed with back to audience.* BESSIE *opens a music-book; and they gather about her, turning over the leaves.* PATIENCE *sits on lounge,* L.

*Patience.* Thoughtless girls! they lack the wisdom

and ripe ex-ex — Dear me! it's so hard to remember
these words! — experience of my ma-ma — older years.
But I, in what the poet calls "the fresh bloom of
womanhood," can curb their flightiness. Ah, this life
is so con-con-gealing to my ambitious spirit! I am so
rapidly mastering the ru-ru — first steps of learning!
I feel that I shall de-de-velop a gi-gi-*antic* mind, and
burst upon the rude boors of Razorly like some glorious starry con-con-consternation.

(*Enter* JOB, R., *with a large quarto dictionary in his
arms. He stops at entrance; sees* PATIENCE, *clasps
the dictionary to his breast, and heaves a sigh.*)

*Maria* (*at piano*). Hush! there's Job. Now watch
the pair.

*Job.* There she is, "a-sittin' on the style, Mary,"
the stylish lounge. Oh, would I were the plush upon
that lounge, that I might clasp that form! That's
Romeo, altered for the occasion. Oh, I'm chock full
of these frenzied ideas! I do nothing but read Shak-
speare and them other poet-chaps — when I ain't hand-
dling plates, or scouring knives; for I'm in love, oh,
so bad! with Patience Plunkett. Oh that name! it
runs in my head. It is so musical, so full of poetry!

> With fair, bewitching Patience Plunkett
> I'm in love. Who would have thunk it?

There's poetry, all out of my own head too. (*Comes
down.*) Miss Patience! dear Patience!

*Patience.* Why, Job, is that you? How you
startled me! I was rume-rume —

*Job.* Not rheumatic. Oh, don't say that you are suffering, beloved Patience!

*Patience.* I was ruminating upon some lines in Homer's *Ilyd*, the original Greek. You are not acquainted with Greek, Job?

*Job.* Well, Patience, I'm not acquainted with many on 'em. There was old Pat Haggerty, in Razorly: they used to call him an Original Greek —

*Patience.* O Job! I have no patience with you. How can you expect me to stoop from my high speer to mate with you, unless you cultivate your head more ass-ass-iduously?

*Job.* Well, I've had it cut and shampooed three times since I've been here. If that ain't cultivating it, I'll have it ploughed next time. Here's your dictionary, Patience.

*Patience.* Thank you: I do not require it.

*Job.* Then, why did you send for it?

*Augusta (at piano, reading music-titles as they turn the leaves).* " Wouldn't you like to know?"

*Job (turning round).* Eh? Why, there's the whole lot of 'em!

*Maria.* No: that won't do. That's too sentimental.

*Patience.* They sent for it, not I. You can take it back.

*Job.* O Patience! why are you so cold to one who loves you to distraction? Why —

*Maria (reading title).* " Lubly Cynthia." That's good.

*Job (turning round).* Plague take those girls!

18*

You know that for love of you I've left my home, Patience, and have donned the apron of a waiter, and become a patient waiter for you, Patience. Oh! when shall my love be rewarded with the possession of that plump white hand?

*Jane.* "When Johnny comes marching home." That's lovely.

*Job (turning round).* Eh? Oh, bother them girls!

*Patience.* Don't mind them, Job. They do not dream of our attachment. They do not dream you are my —

*Maria.* "Curly little bow-wow."

*Job (turning round).* There, now! What's the use of trying to talk where them girls are? Patience, dear Patience, meet me, meet me —

*Augusta.* "Meet me by moonlight alone."

*Job.* Oh them girls! Meet me after tea in the woodshed, while I am cleaning knives. We can commune: we can exchange vows: we can —

*Maria.* "Root hog or die."

*Patience.* Yes, Job, I will be there. But be secret. If our attachment is discovered. Mrs. Candor will instantly dismiss you. And it's so romantic to have a lover in disguise! I know you love me, Job. Have patience.

*Job.* I mean to have her. Don't I love you better than all else in the world? better than —

*Augusta.* "My old Aunt Sally."

*Job.* Eh? (*Aside.*) I believe they are doing that on purpose. (*Aloud.*) Farewell, Patience! I must tear myself away from your beloved presence. My heart —

*Maria.* "Oh! my heart goes pit-a-pat."

*Augusta.* "Somebody's coming. I'll not tell who."

*Jane.* "Let me kiss him for his mother."

*Lucy.* "Single gentleman, how do you do?"

*Job.* Eh? Oh, I'm pretty well.

*Maria.* Oh! nobody's talking to you, Job. Go about your business.

*Job.* Thank you. I don't hanker for your society, do I? A parcel of harum-scarum girls, who are no more to be compared to —

*Lucy (reads).* "The girl I left behind me."

*Job.* Oh, gracious! can they suspect? (*Starts off R., drops the dictionary, and stumbles over it; then picks it up, and exit R.*)

*Maria.* He's stumbled over the hard words too.

*Bessie.* There's nothing here we can sing.

*Maria.* Oh! here's one: "Upidee."

*Lucy.* Oh, that's nice! (*One of the girls strikes the piano, and all join in chorus of "Upidee." At the conclusion, three loud thumps are heard outside.*)

*Maria.* Oh, dear! That's Tom. We have disturbed him.

*Lucy.* No matter: let's try it again, softer. (*Chorus repeated. At its conclusion, enter* TOM, R., *with a blanket wrapped about him, and a wet towel tied about his head. The girls scream, and run down* R. *and* L., *leaving him in* C.)

*Tom.* Oh, dear! how can you reasonably suppose that a young man can be comfortably sick with such a racket going on down here? Oh, my head, my head! my poor, poor head!

*Bessie.*  Oh, Tom, we're so sorry we disturbed you!

*All* (*in chorus*).  Yes, indeed; awful!

*Lucy.*  Wouldn't have done it for the world, had we known you didn't like it.

*All* (*in chorus*).  No, indeed, we wouldn't!

*Tom.*  Oh, yes! that's all very well, now the mischief's done.  Why, you might drive me into a fever.

*All* (*in chorus*).  Oh, that would be dreadful!

*Tom.*  You might — you might bring on convulsions, spasms, with such outrageous squalling.  I'll complain of you!  Where's my aunt?  Where is my fond, affectionate relative?

*Bessie.*  She's gone out, Tom: gone to the doctor's.

*Tom.*  Eh?  Gone out?  Good!  (*Throws off blanket, and tears towel from his head.*)  Thomas is himself again!

*All* (*in chorus*).  Why, Tom!

*Tom.*  Because Tom is only homesick, girls.  My good aunt would not give me time to explain that I was tired of school, eager to have a frolic, and so got leave of absence, and came home for a day.  No: she caught the "sickness," and bundled me off to bed.  I humored the joke, and laughed under the bedquilt.  But no sooner was she out of the room, but I was out of bed, dressed myself, and here I am, ready for any thing in the way of sport you have to offer.  How long will she be gone?

*Bessie.*  Perhaps half an hour.

*Tom.*  Then for half an hour we will enjoy ourselves.  Come, girls, what shall it be?

*Maria.*  Oh! isn't this jolly?

*Augusta.* Real nice! ·

*Jane (and others).* Splendid! Beautiful!

*Augusta.* Let's play " Hide the Slipper."

*Maria.* No: " Copenhagen."

*Tom.* Any thing — every thing. The noisier the better.

*Patience (rising).* Stop! Young ladies, are you aware of the rules of this ed-ed-ucational institute? We have been sent here from our happy homes, to be se-se-questrated from contact with the ruder sex ; and now you propose to indulge in games, childish games, for your amusement and ame-ame-amelioration. I am ashamed of you! I blush for you!

*Tom (aside to* MARIA). Oh! that's one of the teachers.

*Maria.* Hush! It's one of the girls.

*Tom.* One of the girls? Why, she's old enough to be your mother!

*Patience.* I shall not submit to the in-in-trusion of a young man upon our privacy. He must instantly leave the room.

*Tom.* I beg your pardon, Mrs. — Excuse me, miss : a slip of the tongue. But you look so much like my Aunt Matilda! But then, she's forty-five ; and you can't be over thirty —

*Patience.* Sir!

*Tom.* Not quite, miss. I'm still very young, and not entitled to that address. But I couldn't think of infringing upon the rules ; oh, no! I should have been pleased to spend half an hour in such agreeable society ; but, as you object, I will go.

*Girls (in chorus).* Oh, no; don't go; stay!

*Patience.* I insist upon his immediately quitting the room. I did not come here to flirt and frolic with young men, but to improve my mind, to store it —

*Maria.* Oh, bosh, Patience! I've no patience with you.

*Tom.* "Let Patience have her perfect work."

*Maria (aside).* She's a humbug, Tom. Our Job is in love with her, and she with him; and they are billing and cooing every chance they can get.

*Tom (aside).* Maria, you're a jewel. You have enlightened my understanding. You shall see some fun. (*Aloud.*) Miss Patience, you are right: I was wrong to disturb your peaceful meditation. Forgive me. I will go, and in the quiet of my chamber contemplate — the basin of gruel which my fond aunt has left me for consolation. — Sorry, girls; but the rules must be obeyed.    [*Exit,* R.

*Maria.* Patience Plunkett, you're a hateful old thing!

*Augusta.* Yes; just as mean as you can be.

*June.* If you are so fond of seclusion, why don't you go to your own room?

*Maria.* Yes; and study the Book of Job.

*Bessie.* Hush, Maria!

*Patience.* You know I am right; and I am not at all stu-stu-pefied by your ob-ob-jaculations. I am a few years older than you — only a few; and I have wisdom to guide —

*Maria.* Oh, fiddlesticks! We have all the preaching we want, and don't believe in yours.

*Tom* (*outside*). Oh, oh! My hand! my hand!

*Bessie.* Tom has hurt himself.

*Tom* (*outside*). Oh! gracious goodness, how it smarts! (*Enters R. hurriedly, his left hand concealed in a large piece of white cloth. He should also have in his hand a piece of wood, under the cloth; a string in his right hand.*) O girls! I've done it now! That hand I was so proud of, oh! so white and delicate, oh!

*Bessie.* What is it, Tom? Have you cut it?

*Lucy.* Burnt it?

*All* (*in chorus*). Oh! what is the matter? (*They gather about him.*)

*Tom.* Oh! don't come near me. The slightest touch is agony, agony, agony! I went up stairs — oh! to my basin of gruel — oh! Beside the gruel — oh! there was a knife — oh! I took it up — oh! and — and — and oh, oh, oh!

*June.* I've got some Russia salve in my room.

*Maria.* Let me run for it.

*Tom.* No. I've spread on the salve an inch thick. Oh! it's all right. It will soon be well. If I only had some one to tie it up for me!

*All* (*in chorus*). Let me. Let me. I'll tie it. (*They crowd around him.*)

*Tom.* Oh, quit! Keep off! Do you want to kill me. The least touch causes an indescribable sensation to quiver and shoot to the roots of my hair. Oh! I want a gentle hand, a skilful hand, a matronly hand. Miss Patience, you have much skill, tact. Will you condescend to — to tie up my paw?

*Girls* (*in chorus*).  Poor Tom!

*Patience* (*approaching him*).  Certainly, if I can relieve your suffering.

*Tom.*  You can, you can!  Oh!  (*Gives her string, and extends his hand.  She stands* L. *of him.*  GIRLS *fall back* R. *and* L.  *She winds the string about hand.*)

*Tom.*  Gently, gently!  Oh! how soft and tender! It seems as though my mother was hovering about me. Take care, take care!  Gently!  (*She ties the string.*) Be very careful.

*Patience.*  I think that is tied tight.

*Tom.*  You think so?  But you must be sure.

*Patience* (*taking his hand, and looking at string*). Yes, it's all right.

*Tom* (*slipping his hand out of cloth, leaving it in her hands*).  Then you keep it, Patience, as a slight token of regard.  "I'd offer thee this hand of mine, if I could love thee less."  Keep it, Patience, and "wipe your weeping eyes," when I am far away.

[*Runs off* R.

*Patience* (*throws the wrapper after him;* GIRLS *laugh*).  Was there ever such an insulting young puppy!  Oh, his aunt shall know of this!  I'll not go to my slumbers until I have told my story.  Now laugh.  (GIRLS *shout with laughter.*)  You ought to be ashamed of yourselves.

*Maria.*  You told us to laugh.  Seems to me you cannot be suited any way.

*Patience* (*sits on lounge*).  That scamp shall go out of this house. or I will.  The idea of his daring to play such a trick upon me!  Thought his mother was hovering about him!

(*Enter* Tom R., *enveloped in a large cloak or "water-proof," straw bonnet on his head, with a green veil down.*)

*Tom* (*at* R.). Ef yez plaise, young ladies, I'm a poor ould widdy-woman, wid a husband in Californy; and the door was open, and I made bould, ef yez plaise, to walk in, and beg a chrust of bread. It's nine days jist, since a morsel of bread, or a sup of tay, has passed me lips.

*Bessie.* Poor old lady!

*Chorus.* Oh! do come in! (BESSIE *sets a chair* C., *and the others crowd about* TOM, *and lead him to chair.*)

*Tom.* Oh! it's the kind hearts yez have, ony way. I'm wairy wid the walkin', and faint wid the hunger; and I've corns on my fute, and chilblain on my fingers, an' siven childer at home.

*Maria.* Somebody give her something to eat.

*Jane.* Here's Job with the tray.

*Augusta.* And our lunch. (*Enter* Job *with tray.*)

*Job.* Hallo! Who's this?

*Jane.* A poor old woman, nearly starving. Quick! Give me the tray. (*Takes it, and places it in* Tom's *lap.*) Here, old woman, help yourself.

*Tom* (*aside*). My eyes! Here's luck; and I've had nothing but gruel. (*Eats voraciously.*) It's the kind hearts ye have.

*Jane.* Poor thing. Hasn't eaten any thing for nine days!

*Job.* I should say nine months, — the way she puts it away.

19

*Maria.* Oh, there's Bridget! Here, Bridget! (*Enter* BRIDGET, R.) Here's a countrywoman of yours.

*Bridget.* Indade! An' what be she doin' up-stairs, I dunno?

*Bessie.* She's very hungry, and we gave her our lunch.

*Bridget.* Oh, murther! An' me company mince-pies goin' down her throat! Oh! it's wastin' yez are. A cowld pratie would be good enough for her.

*Maria.* Speak to her, Bridget; the tongue of her native land might please her.

*Bridget.* Faith, it's my belief that the Yankee tongue she's stowin' away is far more to her liking. Whist, avourneen!

*Tom* (*aside*). That's Irish. (*Aloud.*) To be sure! Yis, siscon. Fag-a-Balah. Erin-go-bragh. I'm obleeged to yez.

*Bridget.* Were yez long from the owld country?

*Tom.* Siventeen years come nixt Candlemas.

*Bridget.* County Tipperary, I dunno?

*Tom* (*aside*). Nor I either. (*Aloud.*) County Coberdowelgowen. D'ye mind that?

*Bridget.* 'Pon my sowl, I niver heard of it. D'ye know Larry McFinley at all, at all?

*Tom.* Him as lived at Doublin?

*Bridget.* Thrue for yez.

*Tom.* 'Pon me sowl, I niver hard his name before or since. My memory's failin', since I took to fortin'-tellin'.

*Girls* (*in chorus*). Oh! a fortune-teller. Isn't that grand!

*Job.* Well, old lady, if you're done with that waiter, I'll take it.

*Tom (giving waiter).* It's little appetite I have, any way.

*Job.* Little! She *has* done with it. There's nothing left.

*Tom.* Yis. I'm a bit of a fortin'-teller; and, in return for yer kindness, I'll be after tellin' yez a bit.

*Maria.* Tell me mine first.

*Other girls.* No, no! Mine, mine!

*Tom.* Ah, be aisy. The wisest and the wittiest afore the youngest and the prettiest, that's my way.

*Job.* Well, 'sposin' you commence with me, old lady. I calculate I can see through a grindstone when there's a hole in it.

*Tom.* Ah! but they don't make the holes large enough for your observation nowadays, my foine fellow. But I know you. I can say through yez. Yez not yerself at all. Lave me alone for seein' through a body. You're in love. Ah! don't blush, man: it's rid enough yez are, onyhow. Yer fortune's made, — why would I be tellin' yez?

*Job (aside).* She's a keen one.

*Bridget.* If yez plaise, will yez tell me?

*Tom.* Oh! go way wid yez. Don't demane yerself before the foine folk!

*Bridget (angrily.)* Will, I'd loike to know.

*Tom.* Will, yez won't. It's ignorant yez are. The lady of the house would like to know where the sugar goes! D'ye mind?

*Bridget.* Oh! it's a witch she is, onyhow. I'll not cross her.

*June.* Now, my good woman, please tell me my fortune.

*Other Girls.* No. Mine, mine!

*Tom.* Be aisy. Don't I tell you? There's the foine lady on the sate beyant. Would she be after having her fortune towld, I dunno?

*Patience.* No. I do not believe in such negrominstrelsy.

*Maria.* Necromancy. Oh! what a mistake!

*Tom.* Well, I don't know. The fates p'int that way. Onless I can tell her fate, I'll not be permitted to oblige yez.

*Maria.* Oh, do, Patience!

*Other Girls.* Yes, Patience, do!

*Job.* Yes, do, dear — I mean, Miss Patience.

*Patience.* Well, if it will please you, I will condescend to the examination. (*Approaches* Tom, *and offers her hand. He takes it. The* Girls *crowd about him.*)

*Tom.* Faith, that's a good hand, — a foine large hand; and yez a fortune. You've gowld and galore. (*Enter* Mrs. Candor, *unperceived, at back, with her hat and shawl; she stands by piano.*) Ah! but what's this? Ah! Yis, it's the way of the wourld. There's a young man close by.

*Patience* (*trying to release her hand*). It's no such thing. Let me go!

*Tom.* It's the truth I'm tellin'.

*Job.* She's a-goin' to let the cat out of the bag.

*Patience.* I don't want to hear any more.

*Tom.* Aisy, aisy! It's the fates wills it! He loves

yez, honey, and you love him ; and what will love not
do, honey? He drops from his high estate, puts on
the waiter's apron, and follows you, — his heart all the
time cryin', " Have Patience!" Owld Job, him as
had the cutaneous irruptions, had patience, and so
shall Job Seedling have Patience.

*Girls (in chorus).* Oh. my! Our Job?

*Patience.* No: not your Job, but my Job. I'm
not ashamed to own him!

*Mrs. Candor (coming forward).* I'm very glad to
hear it. (GIRLS *start to* R. *and* L.)

*Girls (in chorus).* Mrs. Candor!

*Tom (aside).* My aunt! Oh, here's a pickle.
(*Hides his head.*)

*Job (aside).* There'll be a nice row now!

*Mrs. Candor (to Patience).* So, young lady, con-
trary to all rules, you are carrying on a flirtation under
my very nose.

*Girls (in chorus).* It's awful! wicked! O Patience!

*Patience.* Well, what is a poor girl to do? Job
loves me, and I love Job; and — and (*sobbing*) you
couldn't be so wicked as to part two-wo-wo young
lovers!

*Job.* Yes; born for each other, —

"Two roses on one stalk!"

Them's us, Patience and Job.

*Mrs. Candor.* You, Master Job, will be wanted
here no more ; and as for you, Miss Patience, a word
with you. (*They go* L., *and talk in dumb show.*)

19*

*Bridget.* Faith, I'll git the owld woman out of the way. (*To* Tom.) Whist, come away! (*Takes hold of him, and shakes him.*) The misthress will be the death of yez. Coome!

*Tom* (*aside*). Away wid yez!

*Bridget.* Away wid yerself, or there'll be throuble whin the misthress claps her eye onto yez. Coome, coome! (*Pulling her.*)

*Mrs. Candor.* Yes, Patience, I think it best you should close your connection with the school at once. (*Turns to* Tom.) But who is this?

*Bridget.* If yez plaise, she's a cousin of mine from County Cob-Cob — something; and, if yez plaise, she's a fortune-teller.

*Tom.* Af yez plaise, would I tell yez fate, misthress?

*Mrs. Candor.* No: let me tell yours. Boys that deceive their elders will never come to good.

*Tom* (*jumps up, and throws off cloak and bonnet*). Discovered!

*Girls* (*in chorus*). It's Tom! Oh, it's Tom!

*Bridget.* Well, I niver! 'Pon my sowl! I dhouted the accint of his muther-tongue. County Cob-Cob! Oh, yez a gay desaver!

*Tom.* It was the gruel, aunt. It flew to my head.

*Mrs. Candor.* Oh, you scamp! Pack up your bag, and off to school at once: you have made a fine disturbance here.

*Tom.* I meant no harm, aunt. I was anxious to come home to taste your mince-pies; eh, Bridget?

*Bridget.* It's a greedy epicac yez are, anyhow.

*Tom.* Your tongue and pickles. You wouldn't give me time to explain, and I was so homesick! Let me stay my time out.

*Girls* (*in chorus*). Oh, do, Mrs. Candor, do!

*Mrs. Candor.* No: back you go. You've given me a fright, made me travel a mile to the doctor's, and set my school in commotion. No, sir; back you go. I'll have no thorns among my roses.

*Tom.* Ah! but I removed the thorns, aunt. I think I'll get back, though. 'Twill be such an item for the papers! — "Romantic episode at Rosebush Institute."

*Mrs. Candor.* Would you ruin me?

*Tom.* Then don't send me away hungry. Stuff me with mince-pies, so that I can't utter a word, and the world shall never know how a homesick youth proved that love, in the halls of learning, is but a Thorn among the Roses.

*Curtain.*

# A CHRISTMAS CAROL.

225

# A CHRISTMAS CAROL.

[Arranged as an entertainment from Dickens's Christmas Story.]

---

## CHARACTERS.

EBENEZER SCROOGE.
JACOB MARLEY, the shadow.
FRED, Scrooge's nephew.
BOB CRATCHIT.
TINY TIM.
BOY.
THE GHOST OF CHRISTMAS PAST.
THE GHOST OF CHRISTMAS PRESENT.
THE GHOST OF CHRISTMAS TO COME.

---

## COSTUMES.

SCROOGE.  Rusty suit of black; gray wig.

MARLEY.  Blue coat with brass buttons; breeches; top-boots with tassels; chain about his waist, with padlocks and keys fastened upon it; at the end, a cash-box; very white face; white wig, with hair standing up.

FRED.  Handsome modern costume; light overcoat; red scarf tied loosely about his neck; gloves; hat.

BOB CRATCHIT.  Rusty blue coat; shabby pants; iron-gray wig; large white comforter about his neck.

TINY TIM.  Roundabout jacket; comforter about his neck; crutch; cap.

227

Boy. Jacket; large cap; very red nose; large mittens; comforter about his neck.

Christmas Past. A little girl; short white spangled dress; white stockings; shoes; a wig of long white hair.

Christmas Present. Purple robe reaching to the floor, trimmed with fur; long, brown, curly hair; full brown beard; on his head "a holly-wreath, set here and there with shining icicles;" a belt around his waist, to which is attached a scabbard.

Christmas to Come. Long black robe, with hood entirely concealing his features.

These costumes can be altered or improved by reference to Fields, Osgood, & Co.'s illustrated Christmas Carol.

Arrangement. This entertainment is arranged for a stage eighteen feet wide by fourteen feet deep. A curtain, to draw up, is required between the audience and the performers. Half way up the stage, another curtain, to separate in the centre, and draw aside: the front curtain should be green, the back dark fabric. The front of the stage represents Scrooge's office, where the dream (in this version) occurs. The back is used for the pictures. For home representation, the same arrangement can be easily carried out. The performer is directed as though standing upon the stage, facing audience.

## STAVE I.

SCENE. —SCROOGE'S *office.* L., *a low desk, at which sits* SCROOGE, *in a large arm-chair.* R., *a high desk, with a tall stool; candle burning upon the desk.* C., *a low stool.* BOB *standing by the desk with a poker in his hand; one foot advanced, as though creeping off* L., *looking at* SCROOGE *with an anxious expression.*

*Scrooge (looking round).* Here, you! don't you do it ; don't you do it! Haven't I told you, that, if you venture to waste my coals, 'twill be necessary for us to part? Haven't I?

(BOB *drops the poker, gets upon stool, and tries to warm his hands at the candle.*)

*Fred (outside,* R.). A merry Christmas, uncle! Ha, ha, ha! (*Enters* R.) A merry Christmas! God save you!

*Scrooge.* Bah! humbug!

*Fred.* Christmas a humbug, uncle? You don't mean *that,* I'm sure.

*Scrooge.* I do. Out upon merry Christmas! What's Christmas-time to *you* but a time for paying bills without money, — a time for finding yourself a year older, and not an hour richer? Bah! If I had my will, every idiot who goes about with "Merry Christmas" on his lips should be boiled with his own pudding, and burned with a stake of holly through his heart, he should.

20

*Fred.* Uncle!

*Scrooge.* Nephew, keep Christmas in your own way, and let me keep it in mine.

*Fred.* Keep it! But you don't keep it.

*Scrooge.* Let me leave it alone, then. Much good may it do you! Much good it has ever *done* you.

*Fred.* There are many good things, from which I might have derived good, by which I have not profited, I dare say Christmas among the rest. But I am sure I have always thought of Christmas-time when it has come round, apart from the veneration due to its sacred origin (if any thing belonging to it can be apart from that), as a good time, — a kind, forgiving, charitable, pleasant time, — the only time I know of in the long calendar of the year when men and women seem, by one consent, to open their shut-up hearts freely, and to think of people below them as if they really were fellow-travellers to the grave, and not another race of creatures, bound on other journeys. And therefore, uncle, though it has never put a scrap of gold or silver in my pocket, I believe that it has done me good, and *will* do me good; and I say, God bless it! (Bob *claps his hands heartily.*)

*Scrooge.* Let me hear another sound from you, and you'll keep your Christmas by losing your situation. (*To* Fred.) You're quite a powerful speaker, sir. I wonder you don't go into Parliament.

*Fred.* Don't be angry, uncle. Come, dine with us to-morrow.

*Scrooge.* I'll see you — (Bob *sneezes violently.*) What's the matter with *you?*

*Fred.* Come, uncle; say " Yes."

*Scrooge.* No.

*Fred.* But why? why?

*Scrooge.* Why did you get married?

*Fred.* Because I fell in love.

*Scrooge.* Because you fell in love! (*Suddenly turns to his desk.*) Good afternoon.

*Fred.* Nay, uncle, you never came to see me before that happened. Why give it as a reason for not coming now?

*Scrooge.* Good afternoon.

*Fred.* I want nothing from you: I ask nothing from you. Why cannot we be friends?

*Scrooge.* Good afternoon.

*Fred.* I am sorry, with all my heart, to find you so resolute. But I have made the trial, in homage to Christmas; and I'll keep my Christmas humor to the last. So a merry Christmas, uncle!

*Scrooge.* Good afternoon.

*Fred.* And a happy new year!

*Scrooge.* Good afternoon.

*Fred* (*turns to* R.) Bob Cratchit, a merry Christmas!

*Bob* (*shakes* FRED's *hand*). A merry Christmas, sir. God bless it!

*Fred.* Ay, God bless it! and a happy new year.

*Bob.* And a happy new year, sir; God bless that too!

*Fred.* Ay, ay, Bob; God bless that too. [*Exit,* R.

*Scrooge.* Here, you!

*Bob* (*jumping off stool*). Yes, sir.

*Scrooge.* You'll want all day to-morrow, I suppose?

*Bob.* If quite convenient, sir.

*Scrooge.* It's not convenient, and it's not fair. If I was to stop half-a-crown for it, you'd think yourself mightily ill-used, I'll be bound.

*Bob.* Yes, sir.

*Scrooge.* And yet you don't think me ill-used, when I pay a day's wages for no work.

*Bob.* It's only once a year, sir.

*Scrooge.* A poor excuse for picking a man's pocket every twenty-fifth day of December. Well, you can't have it.

*Bob.* But, sir —

*Scrooge.* You can't have it. I shall expect you here earlier to-morrow.

*Bob.* But, sir —

*Scrooge.* No more. Go! (Bob, *with a very rueful face, puts on his hat, looks at* Scrooge, *and goes slowly out* R.)

*Scrooge* (*turns his chair round to face* C.) There's another fellow, my clerk, with fifteen shillings a week, and a wife and family, talking about a " merry Christmas!" I'll retire to Bedlam. I don't make merry myself at Christmas, and I can't afford to make idle people merry. I help to support the prisons and the workhouses. They cost enough, and those who are badly off can go there. Merry Christmas! Pooh! bah! humbug, humbug! (*Bell rings* R., *bell rings* L., *and then* R. *and* L. *together.*) Mercy! what's that? (*Music, piano, slow and solemn. Enter* R., Marley, *dragging his chain, moving slow. Stops* C., *looking at*

SCROOGE ; *a bandage of white cloth, passing under his jaws, tied on top of his head.*)  How now?  What do you want with me?

*Marley.*  Much.

*Scrooge.*  Who are you?

*Marley.*  Ask me who I *was.*

*Scrooge.*  Who *were* you, then?

*Marley.*  In life, I was your partner, Jacob Marley.

*Scrooge.*  Can — can you sit down?

*Marley.*  I can.

*Scrooge.*  Do it, then.  (MARLEY *sits on stool, c., facing* SCROOGE.)

*Marley.*  You don't believe in me.

*Scrooge.*  I don't.

*Marley.*  What evidence would you have of my reality, beyond that of your senses?

*Scrooge.*  I don't know.

*Marley.*  Why do you doubt your senses?

*Scrooge.*  Because a little thing affects them.  A slight disorder of the stomach makes them cheats. You may be an undigested blot of beef, a bit of mustard, a crumb of cheese, a fragment of an underdone potato.  There's more of gravy than grave about you, whatever you are.  (MARLEY *takes the bandage from his head; his jaw drops.*)  Mercy!  Dreadful apparition, why do you trouble me?  Why do spirits walk the earth? and why do they come to me?

*Marley.*  It is required of every man, that the spirit within him should walk abroad among his fellow-men, and travel far and wide ; and, if that spirit goes not forth in life, it is condemned to do so after death.  My spirit never walked beyond the counting-house. Mark me! in life my spirit never moved beyond the narrow limits of our money-changing hole; and weary journeys lie before me.

*Scrooge.* Seven years dead, and travelling all the time! You travel fast.

*Marley.* On the wings of the wind.

*Scrooge.* You might have got over a great quantity of ground in seven years.

*Marley.* Oh, blind man! blind man! not to know that ages of incessant labor by immortal creatures for this earth, must pass into eternity before the good of which it is susceptible is all developed; not to know that no space of regret can make amends for one life's opportunities misused. Yet I was like this man. I once was like this man.

*Scrooge.* But you were always a good man of business, Jacob.

*Marley.* Business! Mankind was my business. The common welfare was my business. Charity, mercy, forbearance, benevolence, were all my business. Hear me; my time is nearly gone.

*Scrooge.* I will; but don't be hard upon me. Don't be flowery, Jacob, pray.

*Marley.* I am here to-night, to warn you that you have yet a chance and hope of escaping my fate; a chance and hope of my procuring, Ebenezer.

*Scrooge.* You were always a good friend to me. Thank'ee.

*Marley* (*rising*). You will be haunted by three spirits.

*Scrooge.* Is that the chance and hope you mentioned, Jacob? I — I think I'd rather not.

*Marley.* Without their visits you cannot hope to shun the path I tread. Expect the first to-night, when the bell tolls one. Expect the second to-morrow night at the same hour; the third upon the next night, when the last stroke of twelve has ceased to vibrate. Look to see me no more; and look that, for your own sake, you remember what has passed between us. (*Music as before.* MARLEY *walks backward to* R.. *followed by* SCROOGE, *with the same slow step.* MARLEY *goes off* R. *As* SCROOGE *reaches the* R., *bell tolls one: he turns. At the same moment, the* SPIRIT OF CHRISTMAS PAST *appears,* C., *entering at the opening in back curtain.*)

*Scrooge.* Are you the spirit whose coming was foretold to me?

*Spirit.* I am.

*Scrooge.* Who and what are you?

*Spirit.* I am the Ghost of Christmas Past.

*Scrooge.* Long past?

*Spirit.* No: your past. The things that you will see with me are shadows of the things that have been. They will have no consciousness of us.

*Scrooge.* What business brought you here?

*Spirit.* Your welfare. Look! (*Steps* L., SCROOGE R. *Music. The back curtains are drawn, showing a boy sitting at a desk,* R., *with an open book before him.*)

*Scrooge.* It is myself. (*A man dressed as* ALI BABA, *with an axe across his shoulder, passes slowly and noiselessly across stage back of desk,* R. *to* L.)

Why, it's Ali Baba! It's dear, old, honest Ali Baba. Yes, yes; I know. One day, Christmas-time, when yonder solitary child was left here all alone, he *did* come here the first time, just like that poor boy. (ROBINSON CRUSOE, *with a parrot perched upon his finger, crosses from* R. *to* L. *For costumes, the performers can consult the picture-books.*) There's Robinson. There's the parrot, — green body and yellow tail, with a thing like a lettuce growing out of the top of his head; there he is. Poor Robin Crusoe, he called him, when he came home after sailing round the island. "Poor Robin Crusoe! Where have you been, Robin Crusoe?" Ah! poor boy, poor boy! (*Curtain closes.*) I wish (*puts his hand in his pocket*) — but it's too late now.

*Spirit.* What is the matter?

*Scrooge.* Nothing, nothing. There was a boy singing a Christmas carol at my door last night. I should like to have given him something. That's all.

*Spirit.* Let us see another Christmas.

(*Curtains are drawn, disclosing* "FEZZIWIG'S *Dance.*" R., *sits an old lady in cap and spectacles, her hands raised in admiration;* C., *is* FEZZIWIG, *in the act of* "*cutting.*" *He is a large man; white stockings, knee-breeches, shoes with buckles, long white waistcoat, brown coat, large white cravat, and wig. He stands upon his toes, with feet crossed, his countenance radiant with enjoyment. Opposite him,* MRS. F., *as though dancing, one hand on her waist, the other above her head; bright petticoat, dress tucked* up, cap, and gray wig. R. and L. of this couple, three young women and three young men; costumes same as MR. and MRS. FEZZIWIG, with the exception of the wig. They stand leaning forward, with their hands together, as though applauding. In front of FEZZIWIG, a little boy, imitating FEZZIWIG. Behind all, a musician, standing in a chair, in the act of fiddling; music (violin), "Sir Roger de Coverley." The characters should be all ready, and take their places, instantly the curtain falls on the precious picture, as the time is very short.)

*Scrooge.* Why, it's Fezziwig, — bless his old heart ! — my master Fezziwig alive again ; and there's Dick Wilkins, to be sure. He was very much attached to me, was Dick. Poor Dick ! Dear, dear ! those were happy times. How grateful we were ! (*Curtains close on picture.*)

*Spirit.* A small matter, to make these silly people so full of gratitude.

*Scrooge.* Small ?

*Spirit.* Why. is it not ? He has spent but a few pounds of your mortal money, — three or four. perhaps. Is that so much, that he deserves this praise ?

*Scrooge.* It isn't that, Spirit. He has the power to make his people happy or unhappy, — to make their service light or burdensome, a pleasure or a toil. The happiness he gives is quite as great as though it cost a fortune.

*Spirit.* What is the matter ?

*Scrooge.* Nothing particular.

*Spirit.* Something. I think.

*Scrooge.* No, no. I should like to be able to say a word or two to my clerk just now: that's all.

*Spirit.* My time grows short. Quick!

(*Curtains are drawn, disclosing a young girl sitting upon a lounge. Beside her a young man stands, with his arms folded. She is looking away, he looking down at her. Costumes same as in "* FEZZIWIG'S *Dance."*)

*Scrooge.* Again myself.

*Spirit.* Listen.

(*The characters in the picture speak, with soft music while they are speaking.*)

*Girl.* It matters little — to you, very little. Another idol has displaced me; and if it can cheer and comfort you in time to come, as I would have tried to do, I have no just cause to grieve.

*Youth.* What idol has displaced you?

*Girl.* A golden one. You fear the world too much. I have seen your noble aspirations fall off, one by one, until the master passion — gain — engrosses you; have I not?

*Youth.* What then? Even if I have grown so much wiser, what then? I am not changed towards you. Have I ever sought release from our engagement?

*Girl.* In words, no. Never.

*Youth.* In what, then?

*Girl.* In a changed nature; in an altered spirit; in another atmosphere of life, another hope as its great end. If you were free to-day, to-morrow, yesterday, can even I believe that you would choose a dowerless girl? or, choosing her, do I not know that your repentance and regret would surely follow? I do; and I release you, with a full heart, for the love of him you once were.

*Scrooge.* Spirit, remove me from this place.

*Spirit.* I told you these were shadows of the things that have been. That they are what they are, do not blame me.

*Scrooge.* Away, I say! I cannot bear it. Leave me. Away, away! Haunt me no longer! (*Falls into chair, L., and covers his face with his hands. The* SPIRIT *stands at the side of his chair, pointing at the picture. The front curtain slowly descends.*)

## STAVE TWO.

*Lively music. Curtain rises, showing* SCROOGE's *office, as before.* SCROOGE *sitting in chair, looking at back stage, the curtains of which are drawn, disclosing the* GHOST OF CHRISTMAS PRESENT, *who sits upon a seat covered with red, his right arm leaning upon a barrel. In his lap is a bowl of steaming punch; in his left hand, a torch [red fire, such as is used in tableaux, placed in a hollow at the end of a stick, will produce the desired effect]; round him are strewn articles, such as are given for presents. After a few seconds,* CHRISTMAS PRESENT *rises, and comes forward. The curtains close.*

*Spirit.* Look up, look up, and know me better, man. I am the Ghost of Christmas Present. Look upon me. (SCROOGE *slowly rises, and moves round him, looking closely at him. Music continues. This is to give an opportunity to set the stage for the next picture.*) You have never seen the like of me before?

*Scrooge.* Never.

*Spirit.* Have never walked forth with the younger members of my family; meaning (for I am very young) my elders born in these later years?

*Scrooge.* I don't think I have. I'm afraid I have not. Have you had many brothers, Spirit?

*Spirit.* More than eighteen hundred.

*Scrooge.* A tremendous family to provide for. Spirit, show me what you will. Last night I learnt a lesson which is working now. To-night, if you have aught to teach me, let me profit by it.

*Spirit.* Look well upon the pictures I disclose.

[SPIRIT *retires* R., SCROOGE, L.

(*Curtains open, disclosing* " BOB CRATCHIT'S *Christmas.*" *Table,* C., *covered with white cloth; plates.* L. *of table sits* MARTHA, *a young lady about eighteen; brown dress, white collar and cuffs; hair neatly arranged. Beside her, a boy of ten; jacket, with an enormous dickey and black cravat; his hands raised and clasped.* R. *of table, a boy, with a large ruffled collar; his fork in his mouth. Next him, a girl of eight, with her spoon thrust into her mouth. At the further corner of table,* R., *sits* BOB CRATCHIT, *with* TINY TIM *sitting upon his knee.* MRS. CRATCHIT, *dressed in plaid, stands at back of table, holding in both hands a plate bearing a plum-pudding, rather small, with a bunch of holly stuck in the top of it, and alcohol blazing around it. All eyes are fixed upon the pudding. Expression upon the faces joyful and expectant. Music lively.*)

*Scrooge.* It's my clerk, Bob Cratchit.

*Spirit.* Ay, Bob Cratchit, who pockets on Saturdays but fifteen copies of his Christian name; and yet the Ghost of Christmas Present blesses his four-roomed house with the sprinklings of his torch.

*Bob Cratchit* (*raising a cup*). A merry Christmas to us all, my dears! God bless us!

*All* (*in picture*). God bless us!

*Tiny Tim.* God bless us, every one! (*Curtain closes.*)

*Scrooge.* Spirit, tell me if Tiny Tim will live.

*Spirit.* I see a vacant seat in the poor chimney-corner, and a crutch without an owner, carefully preserved. If these shadows remain unaltered by the future, the child will die.

*Scrooge.* No, no! Oh, no, kind Spirit; say he will be spared.

*Spirit.* If these shadows remain unaltered by the future, none other of my race will find him here. What then? If he be like to die, he had better do it, and decrease the surplus population.

*Scrooge.* My very words, when I was asked to give a trifle for the poor!

*Spirit.* Man, — if man you be in heart, not adamant, — forbear that wretched cant until you have discovered what the surplus is, and where it is. Will you decide what men shall live, what men shall die? It may be, that, in the sight of Heaven, you are more worthless, and less fit to live, than this poor man's child.

*Scrooge.* He must live! he must live! Poor Bob! poor Bob!

*Spirit.* Come; look upon another picture.

(*Music lively. Curtain rises upon picture of " Blind Man's Buff at NEPHEW FRED'S." Characters in full evening costume, — gentlemen, white vests and white ties, black clothes; ladies, rich and tasty. In the c. stands a gentleman, blindfolded, leaning forward, groping with his hands, the right hand just touching a young lady, who is half turned from him, but who is looking back with a smile upon her face. Beside her stands a gentleman with his finger upon his lip. Behind the blindfolded gentleman, NEPHEW FRED, with his head thrown back, his mouth open, as though laughing. On the L., a young lady, leaning forward, with her fan to her lips; next her, a gentleman, holding the blindfolded gentleman by the coat-tail, his other hand upon his side, his head thrown back, and mouth open, as though laughing. A boy in front of the party, on his knees, with finger pointing up to the blindfolded gentleman.)*

*Scrooge.* Fred's house!

*Spirit.* Ay, your nephew, making merry. If you listen, you will hear him say of his Uncle Scrooge, "He may rail at Christmas till he dies; but he can't help thinking better of it — I defy him — if he finds me going there in good temper, year after year, and saying, 'Uncle Scrooge, how are you?'"

*Scrooge.* And I refused his invitation, — I refused it! I couldn't do it again, if I had the chance. O Fred, Fred! A merry Christmas, and God bless you!

*(Front curtain descends quickly.)*

## STAVE THREE.

*SCROOGE'S office, as before. Back curtains drawn. The* GHOST OF CHRISTMAS FUTURE *standing*, R., *pointing down;* SCROOGE *beside him*, L. *Mournful music.*

*Scrooge.* Ghost of Christmas Yet to Come, Ghost of the Future, I fear you more than any spectre I have seen; but as I know your purpose is to do me good, and as I hope to live to be another man from what I was, I have borne you company, and did it with a thankful heart. Spectre, something informs me that our parting moment is at hand. I know it, but I know not how. Tell me who that man was with the covered face, whom we saw lying dead, of whom the merchants in the street spoke so carelessly, at whom the vultures of the dead sneered and jested. (*The* SPIRIT *raises his hand, then points behind him.*) Before I draw near to that stone to which you point, answer me one question. Are these the shadows of the things that will be? or are they shadows of things that *may* be, only? (*The* SPIRIT *points as before.*) Men's courses will foreshadow certain ends, to which, if persevered in, they must lead; but, if the courses be departed from, the ends will change. Say it is thus with what you show me. (*The* SPIRIT *moves to* R., *turns, and points to back, where a gravestone leans against the wall, lettered "* EBENEZER SCROOGE." *The position of the* SPIRIT *should hide it till this.* SCROOGE *staggers back till he reaches chair*, L.) Am I that man who lay upon the bed? No, Spirit! Oh, no, no! Spirit, hear me!

I am not the man I was. I will not be the man I must have been but for this intercourse. Why show me this, if I am past all hope? Assure me that I yet may change these shadows you have shown me, by an altered life. (*The* Spirit *slowly lets his hand drop by his side.*) I will honor Christmas in my heart, and try to keep it all the year. I will live in the past, the present, and the future. The spirits of all these shall strive within me. I will not shut out the lessons that they teach. Oh, tell me I may sponge away the writing on this stone! (*Sinks into chair. The curtains slowly close. Bells outside ringing a merry peal. Music lively.* Scrooge *starts from his chair.*) What's this, my own office! (*Runs across stage.*) Hallo! what's to-day?

*Boy* (*outside*, R.). Eh?

*Scrooge.* What's to-day, my fine fellow?

*Boy* (*outside*, R.). To-day? Why, Christmas Day.

*Scrooge* (*dancing about*). It's Christmas Day. I haven't missed it. Hallo, my fine fellow!

*Boy* (*entering*, R.). Hallo!

*Scrooge.* Do you know the poulterer's, in the next street but one, at the corner?

*Boy.* I should hope I did.

*Scrooge.* An intelligent boy; a remarkable boy! Do you know whether they've sold the prize turkey that was hanging up there? Not the little prize turkey, the big one.

*Boy.* What! the one as big as me?

*Scrooge* (*rubbing his hands*). Ha, ha, ha! What a delightful boy! It's a pleasure to talk to him. Yes, my buck.

21*

*Boy.* It's hanging there now.

*Scrooge.* Is it? Go and buy it.

*Boy (with finger to his nose).* Walk-er.

*Scrooge.* No, no: I am in earnest. Go and buy it, and tell 'em to bring it here, that I may give them the directions. Come back with the man, and I'll give you a shilling. Come back with him in less than five minutes, and I'll give you half-a-crown. (*Exit boy in a hurry,* R.) What a delightful boy! See him run! I'll send him to Bob Cratchit's. He sha'n't know who sent it. It's twice the size of Tiny Tim. Joe Miller never made such a joke as sending it to Bob's will be. I forget he's to be here to-day. Oh, if he'd only come late! (*Sits at desk,* L.) Here he is, sure enough! (*Enter* BOB, R., *looking very dejected. Takes off his hat and comforter, and gets upon stool.*) (*Gruffly.*) Hallo! what do you mean by coming here at this time of day?

*Bob.* I am very sorry, sir. I *am* behind my time.

*Scrooge.* You are? Yes, I think you are. Step this way, if you please.

*Bob (getting down from stool).* I'm very sorry —

*Scrooge.* Are you? What do you mean by coming here at this time? Now, I'll tell you what, my man; I'm not going to stand this thing any longer; and therefore (*jumps up, and gives* BOB *a dig in the ribs*) I'm about to raise your salary. (BOB *runs to his desk, and gets a ruler, looking frightened.*) A merry Christmas, Bob! (*Slaps him in the back.*) A merrier Christmas, Bob, my good fellow, than I have given you for many a year. I'll raise your salary, and endeavor to assist your struggling family; and we'll discuss your affairs to-morrow over a Christmas bowl of sparkling bishop, Bob. Home to your family, and have a merry Christmas, and in the morning make up the fires, and buy a second coal-scuttle before you dot another *i*, Bob Cratchit.

*Fred (outside,* R.). A merry Christmas! (*Enters,* R.) Here I am again, uncle.

*Scrooge (running to him, and shaking hands).* A merry Christmas, Fred! I'm going to dine with you.

*Fred.* That's right, uncle. You'll find a merry company.

*Scrooge.* You can't tell me. I know 'em all. My niece, Plumper, the fat sister. Wonderful party! wonderful games! wonderful unanimity! wonderful happiness!

*Fred.* We'll have a merry Christmas.

*Scrooge.* Ay, that we will. Henceforth *I* will honor Christmas in my heart, and try to keep it all the year. I will live in the past, the present, and the future. The spirits of all three shall strive within me. (*Sinks to his knees.*) God bless us all!

*Fred* 
*Bob* } (*sink to their knees*). God bless us all!

(*Music: curtains at back are drawn, disclosing "A Christmas Picture." In the centre, the* GHOST OF CHRISTMAS PRESENT, *seated as before, with his torch raised, red fire blazing in it. At his* L., *the blindfolded gentleman, in the same position as before, with the lady getting away from him; on his* L., *the lady with the fan;* R. *of* CHRISTMAS PRESENT, MRS.

CRATCHIT, *with the pudding in her hands;* MARTHA *at her* R., *with* TINY TIM *in her arms. Two of the children opposite them, looking at the pudding.* TINY TIM *speaks, when curtain is fairly drawn,* " *God bless us every one!*" " *The Christmas Carol*" [see p. 64] *is then sung by an invisible chorus; and the front curtain falls upon the whole picture.*)

www.ingramcontent.com/pod-product-compliance
Lightning Source LLC
Chambersburg PA
CBHW031424020726
47499CB00005B/1580